"How come you never told me?"

His energy sapped, he peered up at Kirsten, realizing she'd cut her hair. The brown waves with hints of cinnamon that once tumbled down her back now barely brushed her shoulders.

Arms crossed, she stared down at him. "Because you'd made it clear you did not want children. It's why we stopped seeing each other, remember?"

He remembered, all right.

"Look, Brady, I don't expect anything from you." She sighed, lowering her arms. "I know you've moved on with your life and I have no intention of interfering. I'm only telling you so you won't be blindsided if or when you see the boys. And now that I've told you, I'll go."

When she turned to leave, he sprang to his feet, startling Daisy. "That's it?" He caught hold of Kirsten's elbow and stepped in front of her. "You tell me I have twin sons and then expect me to carry on as though nothing has changed?" Dropping his hand, he continued to stare at her. "Do you really think I can do that?"

Publishers Weekly bestselling author **Mindy Obenhaus** lives on a ranch in Texas with her husband, two sassy pups, and countless cattle and deer. She's passionate about touching readers with biblical truths in an entertaining, and sometimes adventurous, manner. When she's not writing, you'll usually find her in the kitchen, spending time with family or roaming the ranch. She'd love to connect with you via her website, mindyobenhaus.com.

Books by Mindy Obenhaus

Love Inspired

Hope Crossing

The Cowgirl's Redemption
A Christmas Bargain
Loving the Rancher's Children
Her Christmas Healing
Hidden Secrets Between Them

Bliss, Texas

A Father's Promise
A Brother's Promise
A Future to Fight For
Their Yuletide Healing

Rocky Mountain Heroes

Their Ranch Reunion
The Deputy's Holiday Family
Her Colorado Cowboy
Reunited in the Rockies
Her Rocky Mountain Hope

Visit the Author Profile page at LoveInspired.com for more titles.

Hidden Secrets Between Them

MINDY OBENHAUS

LOVE INSPIRED

INSPIRATIONAL ROMANCE

LOVE INSPIRED®
INSPIRATIONAL ROMANCE

Recycling programs for this product may not exist in your area.

ISBN-13: 978-1-335-93143-6

Hidden Secrets Between Them

Love Inspired
22 Adelaide St. West, 41st Floor
Toronto, Ontario M5H 4E3, Canada
www.LoveInspired.com

Printed in Lithuania

MIX
Paper | Supporting responsible forestry
FSC® C021394

Thine eyes did see my substance, yet being unperfect; and in thy book all my members were written, which in continuance were fashioned, when as yet there was none of them.
—*Psalms* 139:16

For Your Glory Lord

Acknowledgments

To my husband, Richard, thank you
for being so incredibly patient with me.
And to Terri B, lunch is on me!

Chapter One

❧

"You have to tell him."

Standing in the kitchen of the house she'd just signed a six-month lease on, Kirsten Reynolds sighed. "I know, Mom." It was all she'd thought about since Dr. Olson gave her the good news that, despite their concerns of her being a single mother, she'd convinced them she was the right person to run the urgent care center that would soon open in Hope Crossing, Texas.

As a nurse practitioner, the move was a dream come true. Now she had six months to prove herself worthy. Something that, under normal circumstances, wouldn't be a problem. But aside from being a single mom who now lived an hour away from her only support system, there was one more issue standing in the way of her success.

Though climbing Mount Everest might be easier than telling Brady James she now resided in his hometown—along with their four-year-old twin sons. The ones he knew nothing about.

"The boys are content playing with the empty

boxes." Her mother looked up from the carton filled with pantry items to gesture toward the living room where giggles echoed off the bare walls. "Call Brady and see if he's available. If he is, I'll watch the twins while you go talk with him."

Kirsten motioned to the wealth of unpacked boxes. "But there's still so much to do."

Beside the sink, her mother pulled aluminum foil and plastic wrap containers from a box. "Stop making excuses, Kirsten. The quicker you get this over with, the better." She set the items on the counter with a little more force than necessary. "You know, if you would have just told Brady when you first learned you were pregnant, you wouldn't be facing this monumental task now. Brady's a good man. I have no doubt he would've wanted to be involved in the boys' lives."

Kirsten withdrew another plate from its bubble wrap and set it atop the small stack on the stone-looking laminate countertop. While there was no denying her late brother's best friend was an honorable man—"Brady made it very clear he did *not* want children, Mom. If I would've told him, he'd have felt trapped."

"But the two of you had grown so close." Her mother pouted. "Anyone could see how much he cared for you."

Not enough to even discuss the possibility of children.

That had been the deal-breaker in their relationship, so they went their separate ways. A few weeks later, she discovered she was pregnant. Talk about irony.

She'd managed, though. After all, Brady wasn't the first man she'd loved and lost. Cancer had snatched her father away more than a decade ago, then her brother, Scott, was killed in a military training exercise. The only difference was Brady had chosen to walk away.

Nowadays, the only men Kirsten trusted with her heart were the two rambunctious boys enjoying the maze of empty boxes in the other room. Jeremy and Trevor had brought some much-needed sunshine back into her life. And they were the spitting image of their father—thick dark brown hair and ocean-blue eyes. Which was why she'd done away with her personal social media accounts right after they were born.

Yet she'd just moved them to the same small town Brady called home. What had she been thinking?

That heading up your own clinic in a rural area was exactly the opportunity you'd been hoping for.

Not to mention that, despite her determination not to force the boys on Brady, a part of her hoped he might be open to a relationship with them. Her own father had been the sun of her solar system. Now that Jeremy and Trevor were getting older, Kirsten wanted them to have a man they could look up to. Mom's new husband, Kevin, was great about playing with the boys, but that wasn't the same as having a father. Someone who'd teach them those things Kirsten knew so little about. Like how to play baseball and football. How to catch a fish and change the oil in their cars. Not that she was ready to think about the twins driving anytime soon.

Reaching for another plate, she sighed. Five years was a long time. What if Brady had married or was in a relationship?

You're never going to know just standing here.

"Kirsten?"

She jumped. "You're right, Mom." She set the still-wrapped plate aside. "I'm going to go make that call right now." Pushing up her sleeves, she picked her way through the dining portion of the kitchen, maneuvering around boxes until she reached the point where the kitchen, living room and hallway converged. She veered toward the hallway.

"Mama, look."

At Jeremy's voice, she turned.

He stood by himself in the middle of the cluttered living space that had grayish-brown vinyl plank floors, neutral walls and a painted fireplace on the far end.

"Where's your brother?" She started toward him, noticing the closed flaps fluttering on one of the boxes.

"Roar!" Trevor jumped out of the box, fingers held up like claws, his menacing look rapidly morphing into a smile.

Both boys belly-laughed when she squealed and pressed a hand to her chest in mock terror.

"Did we scare you?" Jeremy's hopeful blue eyes peered up at her.

"You sure did." She moved closer and leaned toward them. "Maybe you can get Nana, too."

The twins shared a conspiratorial look, then nodded as she continued to her bedroom at the end of the hall.

She moved past the queen-size bed, which had been set up but still awaited bedding, to stand beside the window overlooking the backyard. The mid-January grass lay dormant with only the occasional speck of green. And while the yard was a manageable size, it butted up to an enclosed pasture that made it look even bigger. Something that had played a role in her decision to rent the three-bedroom, two bath, '70s ranch-style house outside of Hope Crossing proper. Jeremy and Trevor needed room to run and expend energy.

Retrieving her phone from the back pocket of her jeans, she went to her contacts and scrolled until she found Brady's name. What did one say to someone they hadn't spoken to in over five years? Someone who had no idea he'd fathered two beautiful boys.

Her chest squeezed, but she dialed before she

could talk herself out of it. After three rings, she was ready to hang up. Then—

"Hello? Kirsten?" His voice, her name on his lips, was as inviting as a cozy cabin with a roaring fire on a cold winter's night.

She sucked in a breath. "Hello, Brady."

"Wow. It's been a while. How are you?"

"I'm good. Actually, I'm in Hope Crossing. I was hoping we could talk. In person."

His lengthy pause had her pulse quickening.

"Um, sure. Though, in case you haven't noticed, there's really no place to meet in town. No coffee shops or burger joints around here."

Eyeing a large, barren crepe myrtle with peeling bark outside the window, she said, "I can come to you, if you'd like?"

"Okay. Sure. I just got home from work."

"Would now be all right?"

"Yeah—are you okay, Kirsten?"

"Yes. I just have a lot to tell you. What is your address?"

Minutes later, she was kissing Jeremy and Trevor goodbye with promises their grandmother would fix them chicken nuggets and macaroni and cheese for dinner. Then she exited the house and made her way through the cool early evening air to hop into her SUV parked in the two-car drive. She punched Brady's address into her navigation app.

"Arrival time three minutes?" That couldn't be right. Nonetheless, she pulled out of the driveway.

The sun was nearing the horizon, sending shades of gold and orange across the western sky as she headed a few hundred feet in that direction before turning right onto a dirt road. Less than a quarter mile later, she was informed she'd reached her destination.

"You've got to be kidding me." She eased up the gravel drive as the front door opened and a dog trotted out of the charming two-story white farmhouse, followed by Brady. Yet, while the canine continued down the steps, tail wagging, Brady remained on the porch that spanned the breadth of the house. And he remained there, watching as Kirsten parked and exited her vehicle.

At least the yellow lab seemed eager to greet her.

She held out a fist. "Hello, there."

The dog sniffed, tail continuing its back-and-forth movement, before licking her hand in approval. If only things could be that easy with Brady.

As the dog retreated toward the house, the flurry of emotions churning in Kirsten's belly had her second-guessing the sudden impulse to free herself of the secret she'd held onto for far too long.

God, I need Your help. I've ignored Your gentle nudges long enough. I don't want anything from

Brady, You know that. But if he could, please, not hate me, and, maybe, want to be a part of his sons' lives.

With a deep breath, she started in the direction of the man wearing faded jeans and a long-sleeved red pullover, looking every bit as hesitant as she felt. Yet, despite her anxiety, Kirsten found herself smiling as she climbed the handful of steps onto the wooden porch, bringing her even closer to the handsome man she was reminded of every time she looked into the faces of her boys.

"Hi," was all she could manage.

"Hi, yourself." Though the corners of his mouth inched upward, his gaze remained wary.

The dog continued to wag its tail before sitting at Brady's booted feet.

"You look great." He rubbed the dog's almost-white head. Was it possible he was as nervous as Kirsten?

She buried her chilled hands in the pockets of her cardigan. "Thank you. You, too." Funny, she'd never been uncomfortable around Brady before. But then, it wasn't like they were two old friends looking to catch up. He'd trampled her heart. And now she was about to drop a proverbial bombshell.

"I, uh, I'm sure you're wondering why I wanted to see you after all this time. Not to mention what I'm doing in Hope Crossing."

He nodded, his blue eyes riveted to hers. "Just a little."

A chilly breeze had her hugging herself.

As if realizing they were still outside, Brady looked away. "Let's go inside where it's warm." After allowing the dog to enter first, he led Kirsten into a cozy living room with wood floors, a rustic brick fireplace and a chocolate-brown leather sofa with a matching recliner.

"Nice place."

"Thanks. It's a work in progress."

A wet nose touched her hand.

"I'm sorry." She rubbed the canine's head. "I didn't mean to ignore you."

"That's Daisy."

"It's nice to meet you, Daisy." Kirsten's gaze drifted to the glass coffee table laden with what appeared to be signs. *More Service. Less Politics. Brady James for Sheriff.*

She straightened, her gaze darting to his, her insides tangling. "You're running for sheriff?"

"Yeah." Hands in his pockets, he shrugged. "The primary is in May. Some of us aren't real pleased with the fella who took over after Dad retired, so it seemed like the right time for me to step up."

Not when you hear what I'm about to tell you.

While he nonchalantly rocked back on his heels, her mission had just become even more difficult. "So, what was it you wanted to talk about?"

Clearing her throat, she clasped her hands.

"There's a new urgent care center that will be opening soon in Hope Crossing."

"I saw that. Folks are looking forward to not having to make a lengthy drive to find out if they have the flu or just a cold."

"That's good to hear, because I'll be running the center. Which means I now live here in Hope Crossing. Actually, we just moved into our rental house today." She pressed her lips together, willing herself to stop rambling.

"We?" He continued to stare at her.

"Me and my sons."

His eyes widened the way the twins' did whenever they were surprised. "You have kids?"

"Twins."

"Congratulations." His smile was sincere. "You and your husband must be very proud."

She petted Daisy again. "I...never married."

Brady rubbed the back of his neck. "Wow. That's rough. I'm sorry, Kirsten. I'm sure Scott would've had a few choice words for that fella."

"Oh, don't be too hard on him. I never told him I was pregnant."

Confusion lined Brady's forehead. "Why not?"

"Because he didn't want children."

"So you're raising twin boys by yourself. How old are they?"

"Four-and-a-half." Tired of beating around the bush, she heaved a sigh. "Brady, *you're* their father."

* * *

Brady stumbled backward and dropped onto the sofa, his heart beating so fast he thought his chest might explode. Kirsten's last statement had packed more punch than any physical blow. It meant his worst nightmare had become a reality.

Elbows on his knees, he lowered his head to his hands, recalling the night that had haunted him for five years. One that had left him with a multitude of regrets. He had no reason to doubt Kirsten. She wasn't the type to make false accusations. The only thing he couldn't understand was—

"How come you never told me?" His energy suddenly sapped, he peered up at her, realizing she'd cut her hair. The brown waves with hints of cinnamon that once tumbled down her back now barely brushed her shoulders.

Arms crossed, she stared down at him. "Because you'd made it clear you did not want children. It's why we stopped seeing each other, remember?"

He remembered, all right. Because any child of his would've faced a life of uncertainty, wondering when the disease he feared would make itself known and begin waging war on their body and mind the way it had his mother. But Kirsten didn't know that because he'd been too embarrassed to tell her.

"Look, Brady, I don't expect anything from you." She sighed, lowering her arms. "I know you've moved on with your life and I have no intention of interfering. I'm only telling you so you won't be blindsided if or when you see the boys. And now that I've told you, I'll go."

When she turned to leave, he sprang to his feet, startling Daisy. "That's it?" He caught hold of Kirsten's elbow and stepped in front of her. "You tell me I have twin sons and then expect me to carry on as though nothing has changed?" Dropping his hand, he continued to stare at her. "Do you really think I can do that?"

Those big hazel eyes he'd gotten lost in more times than he could count studied him for a moment, while her arms again crisscrossed over her chest like a shield. "I honestly don't know what to think, Brady. I thought I knew you so well. Until you quite emphatically told me you didn't want children."

How he wished he'd been man enough to tell her why. But back then, all he could think about was that he had to end their relationship. Once he'd been discharged from the military, things had quickly grown serious between them. Kirsten made him long for things he hadn't dared consider before. If he hadn't stepped away when he had, he never would've been able to. And he cared too much for Kirsten to burden her with the heartbreak of watching him deteriorate into a shell of himself, the way he and his father had his mother.

Huntington's was a cruel disease that didn't impact only the person who had it; it affected their entire family. And he wasn't about to put Kirsten or anyone else he cared about through that.

Yet, he'd fathered two sons. What if he'd passed the gene on to them?

A heaviness settled in his chest as Daisy whined beside him. He petted the top of her head, wishing this were nothing more than a bad dream. Sometimes reality really stunk.

As the silence stretched on, Kirsten said, "I should go."

"Wait." He moved in front of her, yearning to know more about the boys, yet afraid at the same time. "What are their names?"

"Jeremy Scott and Trevor William."

The significance of those names didn't escape him and made him smile. William was her late father. And Scott wasn't just her brother, he'd been the best friend Brady ever had. It was because of Scott that Kirsten and Brady got together in the first place. The first time she'd traveled to Hawaii to visit Scott when he and Brady were stationed at Fort Shafter, Brady found himself looking for excuses to spend time with her. After she left, they texted or talked almost every day. Later, he was at her side at Scott's funeral, and, once Brady was discharged and had returned to Hope Crossing, he'd made the hour-plus drive to College Station to be with her as often as he could while settling into his job at the sheriff's department.

"I like that you gave them your brother's and dad's names. Gone but not forgotten."

"Never."

Curiosity had his mind tripping over itself with questions. Many he probably didn't have the right to ask. But—"Would you…happen to have a picture of the twins?"

A laugh bubbled out of her. "Are you kidding? I have a phone full of them." She retrieved it from her back pocket, then tapped and scrolled. "Here's one from the other day." She widened the screen with her fingers before handing him the device. "Jeremy's on the left, Trevor is on the right."

A lump formed in his throat as he looked at the two identical boys with dark brown hair and blue eyes, each with an arm slung over their brother's shoulder. Tears blurred his vision. "They—I—" Blinking, he cleared his throat. "They look just like I did at that age."

"That's why I had to tell you now. Before you saw them in public." She darted a finger over the screen to reveal another image. One with goofy faces. Stepping back, she petted Daisy. "You can scroll. It shouldn't take you more than a couple of days to get through all of them." She laughed at her own joke, though he recognized her nervousness.

At least he wasn't the only one who was uncomfortable.

He swiped from one picture to the next, smiling, chuckling a few times. Finally, he looked at her, his insides a knotted mass. "How do you tell them apart?"

She shrugged. "It's kind of instinctive now. I know their personalities. Trevor tends to be more boisterous while Jeremy is more thoughtful—which can be even more dangerous, by the way. You never know what's going on in that sweet little head of his. But when in doubt, Trevor has a birthmark on his left cheek, just above his jawbone."

"Ah, insider secret." Not that he was an insider. On the contrary, he was most definitely an outsider. These were Kirsten's children. He'd turned his back on her. Closing the door so soundly that she hadn't even dared tell him about Jeremy and Trevor.

But that didn't stop the sudden longing in his heart. A longing for something he never knew he wanted.

"Raising one child is hard enough. You have two. How have you managed to care for them?"

"I have a good support system in my mom and stepdad. A job that allows me to afford good childcare." She lifted one shoulder.

He'd like to think he would've helped her, if he had known. What would he have done, though? Would he have married her? Or, at least, had the guts to tell her why he couldn't?

"I guess moving here means losing that support system." Struggling to take a deep breath, he handed the phone back to her. "Where will you be living?"

She puffed out a laugh. "Down the road, make a left at the stop sign and we're on the left."

"The Hart house?"

"Ranch house that backs up to a pasture?"

"That's my pasture," he said with a slow nod. "You'll see my horses grazing out there."

"Ooh." Her brow puckered.

"Problem?"

"The only things my boys love more than horses are dinosaurs. At least dinosaurs are extinct. I'll need to give Jeremy and Trevor a stern warning about staying on *our* side of the fence."

"For their safety, that would be best." A couple of his rescue horses were still skittish. "Though you're welcome to bring the boys by anytime. I'd be happy to introduce them." Rubbing the back of his neck, he wondered why he'd said that. After the way he'd hurt her, Kirsten probably didn't want her boys anywhere near him.

"I'll have to think about that." The way she watched him, though, seemed she was weighing her options. "I need to go." She started toward the door. "Mom has dinner waiting."

He followed. "Carol's here?"

"Just overnight. She runs the office at Kevin's—my stepdad—water well company, and also helps take care of my grandmother, so she needs to get back."

"She remarried, huh?"

"Three years ago."

"I'm sure she'll miss having you and her grandsons close by."

Kirsten continued out the door onto the porch with Daisy on her heels. "You and I both know it's not that far of a drive."

He sure did. Once upon a time, his truck could've made it on autopilot.

After turning the porch lights on, he joined her outside, wishing he could explain why he'd walked away from their relationship. He'd have to eventually. But first he had to come to terms with this new reality. He was a father. And he had no idea how to proceed.

Pausing at the steps, Kirsten buried her hands in the pockets of her sweater. "I meant what I said about not expecting anything from you, Brady. I don't want money or anything like that." Her gaze holding his, she lifted her chin a notch. "But I have two little boys who are growing up faster than I ever imagined, and they need a male influence in their lives." She shrugged. "Who better than their father?"

Their father. He struggled to wrap his brain around the fact.

Before he could respond, she descended the steps.

Daisy started after her.

"Stay, girl."

The Lab plopped beside him with a whine.

Watching Kirsten get into her vehicle, Brady attempted to process what had just taken place. He was a father. Of twins, no less. And while he supposed it was normal for most parents to fear for their children's safety, Brady's fears went beyond scrapes and broken bones.

Kirsten had no idea, though. And she wanted him to be a part of their lives.

Gravel ground beneath tires as her vehicle continued down the drive, red taillights glowing in the darkness, leaving him alone with thoughts of the matching smiles on her phone. Images that would haunt him from now on.

Shoving his hands into the pockets of his jeans, he leaned against the post and stared into the night sky. All this time he thought he'd done the right thing by breaking up with Kirsten. Sparing her from the pain of watching him morph into someone she didn't recognize. Instead, he might have sentenced not only her but her two precious boys to a life of uncertainty. And it was all his fault.

Chapter Two

Feeling as though the weight of the world had settled on his shoulders, Brady pushed away from the post and turned for the door. Despite the turmoil raging inside him, he still had chores to tend to.

Daisy woofed as he reached for the screen.

Brady turned and was blinded by headlights.

Shielding his eyes, he recognized his dad's pickup. Brady let go a sigh. He didn't feel like talking. Especially when it meant confessing his indiscretions. Thankfully, he and his father had a good relationship. Perhaps Dad could help him figure out how to proceed.

Daisy danced in circles beside him.

"Go get him, girl."

The dog raced down the steps.

Moments later, Hank James strolled toward him, wearing a green-plaid-flannel shirt over a pair of well-worn jeans and carrying a large pot. The retired sheriff was now a delivery driver for a local lumber company. Said it still allowed him to work with people, but without the stress.

"I wasn't expecting you."

"Ah, I got a wild hair and made a batch of chicken and dumplings. Thought you might enjoy some." With Daisy at his side, Dad eased up the steps, observing Brady. "What's got you looking so peaked?" The man had always been adept at reading people.

"I had an unexpected visitor."

His father paused beside him. "Who might that be?"

"The last person either of us would expect."

"No idea, but why don't you catch the door and tell me about it?"

Inside, Daisy trailed his father into the kitchen, nose in the air.

Brady closed the door, catching up to them as Dad set the pot atop the gas stove. "I need to go feed the horses."

Dad turned the burner on low. "In that case, let's go. We can talk while we work."

Brady hit the switch for the back porch lights as the three of them moved out the kitchen door and down the back steps.

With Daisy leading them across the yard, Brady said, "Kirsten came to see me."

"Kirsten?" Despite the darkness, he could see the old man's blue eyes widen. "There's a name I haven't heard in a while. What's she doing in Hope Crossing?"

They moved through the gate, gravel crunching

beneath their booted feet as they continued along the drive to the barn.

"She's going to be running that new urgent care center in town." Entering the red metal barn, he flipped on the lights, the aromas of hay and horse enveloping him. Lucy, a dapple-gray mare, waited patiently in her stall, although Brady could hear the other four approaching from the pasture.

"That's an interesting development." The corners of Dad's mouth twitched, and Brady knew what he was thinking. His father liked Kirsten and had never understood why Brady let her go.

"Well, hold your hat. It gets even more interesting." Moving into the combination tack and feed room to his left, Brady snagged the horses' buckets from hooks on the wall before unlatching the feed bins tucked in the corner of the room. "She just moved into the Hart place around the corner." He scooped a measure of feed and emptied it into the first bucket. "Along with her four-year-old twin boys." Repeating the process with another bucket, he noticed his father frowning. Turning, he started across the aisle from the tack room.

"So she's married." The old man harumphed, hastily gathering a portion of hay with his hands before stalking away.

With the feed dispensed, Brady dropped the scoop into the bin before adding supplements and treats to the buckets. Then he stacked them together and joined his father.

"She's not married." Brady set every bucket except Lucy's on the floor outside the mare's stall before continuing inside, passing his father in the process.

"Divorced?" Dad headed for another round of hay as Brady emptied Lucy's bucket into the corner feeder.

He waited for his father to return, preparing himself for the disappointment he was sure to see. "I'm the boys' father."

"You?" Dad stopped beside him, his brow knitting. "That's a twist I wasn't expecting."

Brady slid Lucy's gate closed and moved to the next stall as Nutmeg entered from the pasture through the walkout door. "Me, either."

"You mean you didn't know?"

He could feel his father's gaze boring into his back as he poured the chestnut-colored filly's measure of feed. "Not until about twenty minutes ago."

"How come she—?"

Turning, Brady lifted a hand. "The last time Kirsten and I were together, I made it clear I did *not* want children." Even though he hadn't been a man of faith back then, he'd still been kicking himself for crossing a line he had no business crossing. And talk of kids had been a stern reminder that a happily-ever-after didn't exist for him.

Dad shook his head as he gathered more hay. "You could have at least told her why."

"No point." Brady moved into the next stall. "There's no way I'd put Kirsten through what you and I endured with Mom."

His father appeared at the open gate. "Son, you act as though you have no happy memories of your mother."

Brady shrugged. A few, he supposed. He was only ten when she really started going downhill, so his most vivid memories were of those last four years. And they'd been tough.

Armed with another round of hay, Dad headed for Chief, a bay gelding. "Don't you think Kirsten should've had some say?"

"No." She would've felt trapped, and Brady wanted her to be free to live the life she'd always dreamed of. One with children, grandchildren and growing old with someone she loved.

Conversation stalled as he and his father continued to work, each focused on their tasks, though Brady suspected Dad was sorting through this new revelation as much as Brady was.

Daisy lay on the floor, watching them.

While Dad topped off water buckets and the trough outside, Brady put things away and swept the floor. Then they headed back to the house.

"Any plans to see the boys?" His father plodded up the back steps.

"No. The ball's in my court, I just don't know how to proceed." The screen door creaked as Brady pulled it open. "Kirsten suggested they need a male influence in their lives. And that they love horses, but I don't know."

Under the porch light, his father looked up at him as he pushed the door open. "Well, there you go. You've got horses. Teach 'em to ride."

"I suggested she bring them by so they could meet the horses, but she seemed hesitant."

In the kitchen, Dad headed straight for the sink, rolling up his sleeves. "She's a mom. A single one at that. Being protective is instinctive."

Closing the door, Brady toed off his boots before joining his father.

"I remember the first time I set you atop that Appaloosa we had." Dad soaped up his hands. "I'd never seen your mama so nervous."

"But she loved horses." Brady pushed up his own sleeves.

"I know!" Grabbing a paper towel, his father moved out of the way. "So it's understandable Kirsten would be uneasy."

Brady soaped his hands. It wasn't that he didn't like kids. On the contrary, he enjoyed them. What if they didn't like him, though?

Then again, Kirsten didn't have the support system here that she'd had in College Station. Should he attempt to fill that role?

Dad moved to the stove and lifted the lid on the pot, releasing its comforting aroma. "Those boys deserve to know their father."

Turning off the water, Brady dried his hands.

"But for how long? I remember the confusion and pain of watching a parent deteriorate. I wouldn't wish that on any child."

With a sigh, Dad snagged a ladle from the utensil crock beside the stove and stirred the steaming chicken stew. "At a minimum, you're going to have to tell Kirsten about the Huntington's."

"I'm aware." Brady tossed the spent paper towels in the wastebasket.

"'Course, you could just go ahead and undergo the genetic testing—" Dad glanced his way "—and if you don't have the gene—"

"Aw, come on, Dad. We've talked about this." Brady retrieved two bowls from one of the original wooden cabinets he'd painted a light sage color. "I don't want to know."

Setting the ladle atop the old butcher-block counter, his father faced him. "Not even for your sons?"

"Why? So they can spend their lives wondering when their bodies will start shutting down?" Brady woke up every morning asking himself if this would be the day he'd start having tremors.

Dad's gaze narrowed. "Is that why you're running for sheriff? Just another thing to tick off your list?"

While it was on his list—"You know how I feel about the current sheriff." The man cared more about his political career than the citizens of the county. "And I think I've got a good shot at beating him."

Taking hold of one of the bowls, Dad returned the ladle to the pot and gave the contents another stir before serving them up. "Maybe so. But if you want to make a difference in this world, I can't think of a better place to start than being a father to those boys."

"No. A friend, maybe, but not a father. I don't deserve that. Especially when I may not be around to see them grow up."

"Yet another reason to find out for certain."

"So I can spend my life wondering when it's going to kick in."

Dad handed him the steaming bowl before reaching for his own. "Seems to me you're already doing that. Rushing through life, ticking off a list of things you think you *should* do without really living at all." He filled the second bowl. "Your mother may have left us way too early, but she made the most of the time she had on this earth. Said life was too precious to waste doing something she wasn't passionate about."

Brady stared at his dad. "She said that?"

"Many times. Even as her body started to give way to the disease."

Brady's phone dinged. He moved to the round wooden table opposite the stove and set his bowl down before retrieving the device from his pocket.

When he did, Kirsten's name appeared on the screen.

He opened the text message.

Thought you might like to have this.

Below was an image. The one of the boys with their arms around each other.

"Whatcha got there?" Dad moved beside him.

"Um." Brady cleared his throat. "Kirsten sent me a photo." He passed the phone to his father before slowly descending into his chair.

"Well, I'll be." Dad smiled as he studied the photo. "They're the spittin' image of you." He eased into his own chair, blinking rapidly. After a few moments, he slid the device across the table. "Son, you've got a decision to make. But that right there—" he tapped the phone "—is a precious gift from God. If you can turn your back on those boys, then you're in worse shape than I thought."

"Look, Mom, I've done my part." Kirsten stared at the beach image on the computer screen atop her desk at the urgent care center Tuesday afternoon, wishing she were there. "I told Brady about the twins. I showed him photos. I even sent him one." Because her mother had insisted. "I'm not going to force the boys on him." Though, given the look on his face when she'd shown him that first picture, she was a little surprised she hadn't heard from him. "Maybe he truly is not interested in being a father."

"I'm sorry, Kirsten. I'm having a hard time reconciling the Brady I knew with the one who doesn't seem to want anything to do with his own children."

"I know, Mom. I am, too." How could she have been so wrong?

"Ma'am?"

She turned to find one of the equipment installers standing in the doorway of her succinct office. "Mom, I need to go. Thank you for all your help. Drive safe and we'll talk later." Kirsten had taken the boys to the early learning center today, and her mother spent the morning unpacking while Kirsten began the process of settling in at the urgent care center amid the activity of workmen who'd finished their final touch-ups this morning and the installers who still remained. Now her mother was on her way back to College Station.

After addressing the technician's questions, Kirsten wandered into the small waiting room, smiling as she took in the finished product. The designer had done a nice job of balancing professionalism with a rustic vibe that suited the rural community. The vinyl plank flooring reminded Kirsten of weathered oak and paired well with the dark gray chairs. Large wood-framed images of bluebonnets and grazing longhorns graced two of the light greige walls. But her favorite thing of all was the train wall panel that hung at kid-level near a miniature table with four chairs. The train boasted a variety of animals along with games and activities for little ones. It was the perfect solution for this small space.

Her phone rang and she took it from the back pocket of her jeans, eyeing the Hope Crossing Urgent Care logo over the reception counter. Then she looked at her phone, her heart beating double-time when she saw Brady's name. Was he calling about the boys? Had he decided he wanted to see them? What if he *didn't* want to see them?

Answer it and find out.

She took a deep breath. "Brady. Hi."

"Hey, I need to talk to you someplace private. Would you be available to come by my place later?"

"Sorry. My mom left today, so I'll have Jeremy and Trevor. However, they're at day care and I'm at the urgent care center. There are some guys working but—"

"I really need to talk to you alone." The insistence in his tone had her curious.

"Ma'am?"

She turned as the two installers emerged from the hallway.

"We're done for today. We'll be back around nine tomorrow."

"Oh. Okay. Thank you." She slid a hand into her back pocket, watching as they continued out the door. "Brady?"

"I'm here."

"Strike that. The workers just left for the day, and I don't have to get the boys until later. Can you come by the urgent care?"

"On my way."

She started toward her office to retrieve her insulated water jug, pausing in the restroom to check her look in the newly installed mirror.

Staring at her reflection, she heaved a sigh. "What are you doing? It's just Brady." She flipped off the light on her way out, mentally kicking herself for all but begging him to spend time with Jeremy and Trevor. She probably sounded desperate. What if he thought that was just an excuse? That *she* wanted to spend time with him.

Like that would ever happen. She'd loved and she'd lost. And she wasn't all that fond of losing.

A few minutes later, the chime indicating someone had opened the door had her returning to the waiting room where Brady—clad in his silver-tan uniform—took in the recently revitalized space. It wasn't fair that he looked so good. Seemed he'd only improved with age. On the outside, anyway. The rest was still up for consideration.

"Hello." She continued toward him.

"Thanks for agreeing to meet me."

"I'm glad it worked out." At least she sounded calm.

Once again, his gaze traversed the small space, the corners of his mouth lifting ever so slightly.

"This looks really nice. You'd never know it was once a gas station and auto-repair shop."

"Really?" Her gaze darted toward the door. "So the covered drive out front was already there?"

"Yep. It's where the gas pumps were."

"And I thought they'd added it." *Cut the chit-chat and get down to business.* She cleared her throat. "Would you prefer to talk out here or in my office?" Her desk would make a nice buffer.

"Your office is fine."

Nodding, she started into the hallway. "Can I get you some water?"

"No, thanks, I'm good." He followed her as she veered left at the second door. "When are you supposed to open?"

She motioned to the guest chair before continuing around the sleek cappuccino-colored desk. "Two weeks from yesterday. The rest of the staff will start tomorrow."

Once they were seated, she clasped her hands atop the desk, eager to learn the reason for his visit. "I assume you're here about the twins."

He nodded. "It impacts them, yes." His knuckles were white as he gripped the arms of the chair that matched those in the waiting room. "Kirsten, there's something you don't know about me."

More than him not wanting children? Was he married? In a relationship? And why did her stomach knot as she considered each of those notions?

As if she and Brady would be able to pick up where they left off.

"It's about my mom," he continued.

Her anxiety level dropped a notch. "You were fourteen when she passed away, right?"

"Yes."

"Pneumonia?"

He drew in a long slow breath and let it out. "Yes, but with extenuating circumstances I never mentioned. Something that could potentially affect you and your boys."

Her boys? That alone suggested he had no desire to be a part of their lives.

Perching her elbows on the arms of her brand-new executive chair, she leaned back, hoping to convey a calm she didn't remotely feel. "Go on."

"Have you ever heard of Huntington's Disease?"

"Yes. Though I'm not very familiar with it."

"It's a genetic disease that affects a person's physical, mental and emotional abilities. Symptoms typically appear when people are in their thirties or forties and progressively worsen. Sometimes for decades, sometimes only years." He stared at his now-clasped hands. "My mom's symptoms began appearing when I was around the twins' age. For the next decade, I watched her slowly decline until she was a shell of a person."

"Oh, Brady." Leaning forward, she rested her forearms on her desk. "I can only imagine how difficult it must have been for you to watch her go through that and not understanding."

"I still don't understand why she had to endure that." His gaze lifted to hers. "All I know is that it's genetic."

She mentally sifted through what little she knew about the disease. "As I recall, they have genetic testing for Huntington's. Have you considered that?"

"No."

She glared at him. "Why not?"

"Because I don't want to know. I don't want to fear it any more than I already do."

Her ire grew as she began to put two and two together. Why hadn't he told her this before? "But if it's genetic—"

"And if I have the gene," he cut her off, "there's a fifty-fifty chance the twins could have it, too."

A chill that had nothing to do with the weather settled over Kirsten. "Brady, you *have* to get tested." She needed to know.

"Why? If it's going to happen, it's going to happen. There's no cure. No way to stop it. That's why I didn't want children. And why I couldn't stay with you." He had the nerve to sound remorseful. "You deserved better."

"You're right about that." Rolling her chair back, she stood, her body rigid. "I deserved someone who would've been honest with me. Who trusted me with their deepest, darkest secrets. I *thought* you were that guy, Brady."

"I'm sorry, Kirsten. I knew I was hurting you, but at the time, I thought I was sparing you from something much worse." His gaze met hers. "But if you would have told me you were pregnant, I would have been there for you."

"I want you to get that test, Brady."

He stood, his expression suggesting he was digging in for battle. "No. I don't want to know."

"But *I* do. I have Jeremy and Trevor to consider. If there's a possibility they could get this disease, then I want to make sure they're well cared for." Daring a step closer, she lifted her chin to glare at him. "You can be sure I'm going to research this disease. And if you have even *one* iota of compassion for my sons, then you will get that test."

Chapter Three

Kirsten was right. He was selfish.

Brady had vowed to serve and protect others, first in the military, now as a deputy sheriff. And if things panned out as he hoped, as sheriff. Yet when it came to helping his own flesh and blood, he was shaking in his boots.

While Daisy looked on from outside the barn stall Wednesday afternoon, he lifted Digger's saddle from the divider wall. He couldn't blame Kirsten for going all mama bear on him. Her top priority was to protect her children. *His* children. Strange how he had to keep reminding himself of that fact. Still, the truth had him wondering, could he really continue refusing to test for Huntington's?

He placed the saddle atop the tobiano. Apparently not, since he'd spent half the night staring at his laptop, clicking one link after another to learn more about the disease that had robbed him of his mother, as well as the presymptomatic testing that would determine if he carried the same gene. Which, as it turned out, could be a lengthy process that included counseling and evaluations.

Once he had the straps cinched, he led Digger outside into the bright late afternoon sun.

Daisy spotted a squirrel and took off after it, until it fled up a tree. Then she parked herself at the base and barked up at the critter.

Digger snorted.

"I hear you, my friend." Brady smoothed a hand over the gelding's nose. "I'm looking forward to our ride, too." He needed a little escape from reality.

He was about to climb into the saddle when his phone rang.

Retrieving it from the clip on his belt, he looked at the screen, cringing when he saw Gloriana Broussard's name.

Back in high school, he'd had a crush on the dark-haired beauty who was a year older than him. And she'd used that to her advantage, sweet talking him into helping her release the animals from the school's agricultural barn at the end of his junior year in hopes of getting the ag teacher who'd refused to let her retake an exam in trouble. Unbeknownst to them, the school had installed security cameras and his truck was caught on video.

At the time, he was still struggling to come to terms with his mother's death while his father buried himself in his new position as sheriff. So Brady foolishly went along with Gloriana in hopes of getting her attention. Instead, he'd ended up spending his senior year at a military school. Yet while that turned out to be the best thing that could've happened to him, he'd never quite got over the fact that Gloriana never came to his defense.

Now they both served on the Hope Crossing Fair and Rodeo board, so he supposed he'd better answer.

"Hello." He eyed Daisy, still parked under that tree. At least she'd stopped barking.

"Oh, good. You actually answered."

"And I can hang up just as easily." Why couldn't he let his guard down and treat Gloriana like everyone else?

"But you won't, because this is board business."

He sighed. "Go ahead."

"It's about the Boot Scoot'n Barbecue Bash."

With renovations completed at the Hope Crossing Dance Hall—one of the oldest dance halls in Texas—the board was hosting an event to allow the community a preview of the place that would soon serve as a venue for weddings and other events, providing the board with another source of income.

"Connie Sue Miller was supposed to be in charge of the children's activities," Gloriana continued, "but she's been down in her back since the holidays and is now facing surgery. We need someone to take her place and, since everyone else on the board already has an assignment, I thought, maybe, you'd be willing to take over this one little thing."

And he thought the board had given him a pass because of his sheriff campaign. "What sort of events does she have planned?"

Gloriana was silent for a heartbeat too long. "Nothing. She thought she'd have time once she felt better, but that hasn't happened."

And they were already halfway through January. "Gloriana, I don't know anything about kids."

"Oh, come on, Brady. You were little once. Just ask yourself what you would've enjoyed. It doesn't have to be anything extravagant. Oh! Maybe Alli would have some ideas. Or Tori." Both were former schoolmates, attended his church and worked with children daily, Alli as director of the early learning center and Tori as an elementary school teacher. And they both had kids.

"Why don't you ask them to do it, then?"

"They're not on the board."

He sighed, rubbing the back of his neck. That gave him less than a month to prepare. And he had no idea where to begin.

As silence stretched through the line, Gloriana said, "I'll see if I can secure an interview for you on the local radio station before the primary election." She'd been a television personality in Nashville before returning to Hope Crossing two years ago. Now she worked tirelessly to promote her hometown and, occasionally, stepped in to help its residents. Like when the church youth group was preparing for their holiday fundraiser last month, and someone broke in and stole everything right before Thanksgiving. Gloriana took to the airwaves and the church found themselves inundated with donations and the Christmas Bazaar was a huge success.

"*If* I do the kids' thing?"

"No." She hesitated. "I was going to offer anyway. This just seemed like a good time to throw it out there."

He glanced out over the pasture where his three rescue horses and Lucy grazed. "How come?"

"Because I believe you're the best candidate for the job."

His shoulders drooped. Nothing like being humbled.

"Okay, I'll do it." Even though he had no idea what *to* do. "And I won't turn down the radio gig, but I won't hold you to it, either."

After ending the call, he returned the phone to his hip and climbed atop Digger. This week had started off so well. But ever since Kirsten showed up Monday night, telling him he had twin sons, things had spiraled.

He took hold of the reins. "Come on, boy. Let's ride."

They moved away from the barn at a leisurely pace, Brady tugging the brim of his worn Stetson lower as he perused the land he was pleased to call his own. During his time in the army, he'd been purposeful with his money, tucking away as much as possible with the intention of purchasing his own spread once he returned to Hope Crossing. He wanted horses, and for that he needed land, so he'd lived with his dad for a while after returning stateside until he found just the right place. This little farm had fit the bill. All twenty-nine acres of it.

Now dormant grass spread over the undulating landscape, contrasting with the evergreen live oaks that dotted the property, providing some much-needed shade during summer's heat. This was his haven.

The only thing missing was someone to share it with.

The thought jolted him. And he promptly sent it packing. A solitary life was what he wanted. It made things easier all the way around. Hadn't his recent interactions with Kirsten proved that?

Determined not to harp on the drama of this week, he shook off the notion and continued past the crude metal structure that served as his hay barn, toward the northern edge of his property. "Come on, Daisy. Leave that squirrel alone."

Though the dog seemed torn, it wasn't long before she joined him.

He eyed the fence as he and Digger meandered along, making sure everything was as it should be, and nothing needed repair. Slowly but surely, his knotted muscles began to unwind.

Yep, this was just what he needed. No people. No worries. Just his horse, his dog and a beautiful day.

Continuing along the eastern perimeter, he contemplated the inaugural celebration at the dance hall. What had he enjoyed when he was a kid?

Anything that involved being outdoors. Except that wasn't an option. February weather in Texas was too unpredictable, so this event was confined to the dance hall.

Nearing his southern boundary, children's voices had him jerking his attention away from the fence to scan his surroundings.

Daisy gave a low growl.

"Easy, girl." Finally, he spotted two identical little boys standing on the opposite side of the wire-mesh fence—right behind the Hart house. Both kids were dressed in jeans, one sporting a red jacket while the other's was blue. They were watching Butterscotch, the palomino mare who'd been skin and bones when Brady brought her here several months ago.

Eyeing the ranch-style house behind them, he tugged the reins, bringing Digger to a stop. "Daisy, stay."

The canine whimpered yet complied.

Brady's heart pounded as he glimpsed Kirsten's

sons for the first time. He swallowed around the sudden lump in his throat. *His* sons.

"Hi, horsey." The one in red reached an arm through one of the wire rectangles.

"Horsey," the other one called in a singsong manner.

While Butterscotch ignored them, Brady couldn't look away. His pulse raced. And he felt a slow smile building.

He wanted to get closer. To see them better. But he didn't want to scare them. He was a stranger, after all.

"You guys see that?" he whispered to his companions. "Those are my sons."

Seemingly giving up, the boy in red withdrew his arm. A moment later, he took hold of the fence wire and began to climb.

Brady shifted his gaze to the backyard and the house. Where was Kirsten? If the boys got over the fence, it wasn't Butterscotch Brady would be concerned about. She may be a docile horse, but any animal that felt threatened was unpredictable. And after the abuse she'd endured, she'd scare easily.

With no sign of Kirsten, he gently urged Digger. "Daisy, heel." He didn't want to frighten the boys. Especially when it could cause the one climbing to fall.

"No, Trevor." The one with the blue jacket

tugged the tail of his brother's red one, urging him back to safety.

Brady sat a little taller. Based on what little Kirsten had shared that first night about their personalities, he'd suspected Trevor was the one in red.

He was still several feet away when Jeremy looked in his direction. The kid's eyes went wide, his mouth making a perfect *O* while his brother continued to climb. "Down, Trevor. Come *down*!"

Trevor reached for the wood rail at the top of the fence, looking up as Brady neared. "Whooooa." The kid wobbled. If he let go—

In the shade of a live oak, Brady hastily dismounted and was ready to lunge for the boy when he heard footfalls approaching rapidly from the other side of the fence. Looking up, he saw Kirsten racing toward them, her eyes wide.

"Get away from my son!"

A mother's greatest fear was having her children snatched away. That fear now propelled Kirsten across her backyard at a frenzied pace. Her chest felt as though it might explode. She hadn't even known the boys were outside until she glanced out the window and saw someone trying to grab Trevor.

Whoever was on the other side of the fence raised his hands in the air as she lunged for Trevor. Grabbing him around the torso, she pulled him against her with one arm while reaching for Jeremy with her other hand.

Still breathing hard, she took several steps back. "I don't know who you are, but you'd better—"

"I was trying to prevent him from falling."

Her gaze narrowed on the cowboy. "Brady?"

He lifted his dirty gray cowboy hat long enough to drag a hand through that thick hair of his. "Who did you think I was? I told you this was my property."

Yes, he had. But she hadn't recognized him in that hat. Though he certainly wore it well.

Her cheeks heated as she bit her lip. "What are you doing here?"

"I was checking my fence line when I saw these two trying to get the attention of one of my horses." He motioned to a gold-colored horse moving away from them.

"I only wanted to say hi." Trevor wiggled out of her arms to stare up at her.

Her breathing finally returning to normal, she fisted her hands on her hips and glared down at him. "You can do that from *this* side of the fence."

"Are you a real cowboy?" Jeremy had let go of her hand to shield his eyes from the sun as he peered up at Brady.

He looked down at her son—his son—his expression morphing into something she could only describe as pure delight. "Since I don't own any cows, just horses, I'd have to say no."

"But you're wearing a cowboy hat. Cowboys ride horses." That was Jeremy, always thinking things through.

Brady chuckled. "You got me there, young man."

"He's also a sheriff's deputy." Kirsten again stared at a seemingly put-out Trevor, the corners of her mouth twitching ever so slightly when his eyes widened. Instilling a little healthy fear was never a bad thing.

Turning toward the fence, she said, "Boys, this is our neighbor, Mr. Brady James." She dared a glance his way. The cowboy look definitely suited him. Not that she hadn't seen him in jeans, boots and a work shirt before. But the hat? It rounded out the package rather nicely.

Mentally chastising herself for noticing, she lowered her gaze. That's when she saw the yellow Lab with him. "And his dog, Daisy."

"Can I pet your dog?" Jeremy slowly approached the fence, his little face alight with wonder.

"Sure," said Brady. "Daisy likes to be petted. Careful, though, she likes to lick, too."

Kirsten watched as the boy approached one side of the fence while Daisy waited on the opposite side, tail wagging. "Brady, this is Trevor—" she set a hand atop the daredevil in front of her "—and his twin brother, Jeremy." She nodded to the contemplative boy tentatively reaching through the fence to pet Daisy.

Brady lifted his hat in greeting. "Nice to meet you, gentlemen."

"We're not gentlemen." Jeremy tilted his head to look at Brady, his nose scrunched. "We're boys."

"You sure are." Brady looked like a boy himself. Head tilted slightly, the corners of his mouth lifting as he looked from one twin to the other with a sense of awe.

The reaction made her smile, though she couldn't help wondering what was going through his head. It appeared he was as taken with her boys as she was. And she wasn't sure how she felt about that.

"I want to pet the dog, too." Trevor looked up at her, his bottom lip pooched out. "Can I, Mama? Please?"

"Go ahead."

He raced toward his brother.

"Easy, champ." Brady held out a hand. "We don't run around horses. It might scare them."

Pulling her sweater around her, Kirsten followed at a slower pace. Not because of the horse, but to give her pulse time to return to a normal rate. Ever since she looked out the window, her emotions had been all over the place. Though hearing the twins giggle as Daisy licked their hands was a healing balm. She'd have to make sure they washed up as soon as they went inside.

The saddled horse behind him nickered.

Brady turned. "Sorry, boy. Didn't mean to ignore you." He stroked the pretty paint's nose. "This here's Digger, fellas." He glanced at the boys who stared at the animal, mouths agape.

Trevor gripped the fence wire with both hands. "Can we pet him, too?"

Jeremy craned his neck to look up at Brady. "Please?"

She continued toward them. "Boys, I don't think—"

"I reckon that'd be all right." Reaching for the horse's bridle, Brady turned his gaze to her, those ocean depths challenging. "If your mama doesn't mind passing you over the fence."

He had to be kidding. After what just happened, the boys didn't deserve to be rewarded.

Jeremy turned his hopeful blue eyes to her. "Can we, Mama?"

"Please?" Trevor prayed his little hands together.

She looked at Brady, hoping for a little backup. Instead, he simply lifted a brow.

Holding his stare with a challenge of her own, she said, "After the way you all scared me?"

Jeremy moved toward her, then. Peered up at her with that sweet little face she found difficult to resist. "We sorry, Mama. Me and Trevor didn't mean to scare you." He looked so serious.

Arms crossed, she glanced at Brady, wanting to wipe that satisfied smile off his handsome face.

She was fighting a losing battle.

Lowering her arms, she said, "All right. But if I *ever* catch you boys trying to climb this fence again, I'm going to take all of your dinosaurs for three days."

Both boys' mouths dropped open, their eyes widening.

"We promise," they responded in unison.

With Brady again flanking his side of the fence, she passed Jeremy over the four-foot barrier first.

Picking up Trevor, she encouraged him to look at her. "You listen to Mr. Brady and don't do anything that might scare Digger. Okay?"

"O-kay." Then he hugged her around the neck.

With Jeremy now on the ground beside him, Brady reached for Trevor. He set the boy beside his brother, then crouched to their level while he established a few rules.

Watching him interact with the boys had her battling a score of emotions. A part of her longed for Jeremy and Trevor to know their father and have a relationship with him. But seeing them together unearthed fears she hadn't anticipated. And not only for their physical safety.

What if Brady wanted more than just being a part of their lives? What if he decided he wanted partial custody? Given that she'd kept the boys a secret, a judge wasn't apt to look favorably on her.

Looking away, she sucked in a breath. *Lord, I can't lose them.*

"Mama, look!"

Turning at Jeremy's voice, she spotted the twins standing beside Digger, their little arms stretched high to pet him.

"He likes us," said Trevor.

"That's good." Because the way the horse towered over them made her nervous. "Be sure to stay where he can see you." She didn't want them getting kicked.

Holding the horse's lead rope, Brady approached her. "They're an inquisitive pair."

"Yes, they are."

"What were they doing out here alone?"

Was he accusing her of being neglectful?

Tearing her attention away from the boys, she glared at him across the fence. "We just got home. I'd let them into the house while I unloaded some things from my vehicle, so I *thought* they were inside." Her focus returned to the boys. "Until I looked out the window and saw someone trying to grab Trevor."

"He seemed determined to get to Butterscotch." He poked a thumb toward the blond horse now some distance away. "I didn't want him getting hurt."

"I told you they loved horses."

He perched an elbow atop the fence rail, returning his focus to the boys. "Can't imagine where they get it from. Guess I'll have to teach them a thing or two about riding."

Not on her watch.

Unwilling to allow this unexpected meeting to go to waste, she said, "I don't suppose you've given any thought to what I said the other day, have you?"

He looked her way. "You mean the dictate you gave me?"

She winced. "I suppose I could have been a little less demanding." Once she'd had time to look at things from Brady's perspective—not to mention done a little research—she understood his reluctance. Seemed the majority of people with Huntington's in their family felt the same way he did about the testing. Yet while she tried to put herself in his shoes, she kept coming back to Jeremy and Trevor. "But I hope you were able to view things from my vantage point."

His gaze drifted to the twins. "Until now, my decisions have only affected me. Now I have to consider them."

Them? How could that be? He'd just met the twins.

When he looked at her this time, she saw regret in those ocean eyes that never failed to draw her in. "I'm going to contact my doctor about the genetic testing."

While that was what she'd wanted, his announcement triggered an onslaught of conflicting emotions.

"Be aware, though," he continued, "it's a process that could take a while."

She'd seen that in her research. "I understand." Her gaze met his. "Thank you."

He looked from her to the boys and back again. "Now, there's something I'd like from you."

A thousand what-ifs had her stomach tightening. "Such as?"

Lowering his voice, he said, "I want a relationship with them." He eyed the boys. "They don't need to know I'm their father—not yet, anyway. But I want to get to know them and have them know me. I want to be there for milestones. And I want them to know they can trust me."

She swallowed the unexpected fear threatening to strangle her. The twins were her world. What if Brady tried to take them away from her?

"Kirsten?"

She looked up at him.

"Kids might not have been a part of my plan, but they're my children. I can't turn my back on them."

Of course, he couldn't. And while she longed for Jeremy and Trevor to know their father, until now it had been only the three of them. Suddenly, everything was about to change.

But what choice did she have? She was the one

who'd made the decision not to tell Brady she was pregnant.

She recalled the vegetable-beef soup she'd had in the slow cooker all day. Enough to ensure they'd have leftovers.

"Would you like to join us for supper? I've got some soup and those rolls from a can you used to like so much."

His laugh held a hint of nervousness. Something she, regretfully, found endearing. "They're still my favorite." Rocking back on the heels of his boots, he stared at the boys now playing with Daisy. "Thank you. I'd like that."

"You're welcome." A shaky breath accompanied her words. Hopefully Brady didn't pick up on it.

"What sort of things do they like to do?"

She followed his gaze toward the boys, shrugging. "Run around. Play with their dinosaurs. It varies."

"Sorry, that's not what I meant." He faced her now. "I'm on the town's fair and rodeo board. We're hosting a Boot Scoot'n Barbecue Bash to celebrate the reopening of our historic dance hall."

"Barbecue and dancing? Sounds like fun." Why had she said that? He probably thought she was fishing for an invitation.

"That's what we're hoping." He again eyed the boys. "It's a family-friendly event and I've been asked to come up with something to entertain the kids. Frankly, I'm clueless." Turning back to her, he seemed to wince. "You wouldn't have any suggestions, would you?"

"Hmm." She'd attended plenty of fall festivals and Christmas parties at the boys' day care. "Not off the top of my head. But between the two of us, I'm sure we can come up with something." The words were out of her mouth before she realized she'd just agreed to help him.

Spending any more time than necessary with Brady was a dangerous prospect. One that posed a threat to the life she'd built for her little family. Not to mention the wall she'd erected around her heart.

I want a relationship with them.

If that was the case, then she supposed helping Brady would be the best scenario. He and the boys could get to know each other, and she could keep an eye on Jeremy and Trevor.

Chapter Four

Brady couldn't get back to his house fast enough. After untacking and grooming Digger, he fed the horses and Daisy before changing clothes and driving over to Kirsten's. Seeing Jeremy and Trevor face-to-face, interacting with them, even if it was only for a few minutes, had awakened something unexpected inside him. Suddenly, the desire to know them and be part of their lives had him wanting to make up for the time he'd lost.

The sun had set, and the early evening air was cool as he walked along the sidewalk that led to Kirsten's front door where two little boys greeted him with wide smiles. The sight had his heart pounding.

"Did you bring your horse?" Brady wasn't sure if it was Trevor or Jeremy who'd done the asking, but his guess was Trevor.

"Sorry, fellas, just my truck this time." He motioned toward the driveway.

The boy who'd asked frowned.

His twin, on the other hand, cocked his head

rather thoughtfully. "Where *are* the horseys? And Daisy?" The concern in his eyes had Brady suspecting this one was Jeremy.

"They're having supper in my barn."

"Boys!" Kirsten's voice held a note of panic as she rushed up behind them. "You know you're not supposed to open the door without an adult."

The one he thought was Trevor peered up at her. "Mr. Brady is an adult. He didn't bring his horse, though." Shoulders drooping, the kid turned and retreated.

Just like that, Brady had gone from hero to zero. While he knew from some of his buddies with kids that could be an everyday occurrence, Brady found being dissed right out of the chute rather humbling. How could he build a relationship with the boys if they didn't like him?

With a sigh, Kirsten frowned at the remaining twin. "Jeremy, you know better than to open the door without me."

Brady took solace in the fact he'd been correct in distinguishing the boys.

Jeremy's head lowered. "Sorry, Mama." He wrapped his arms around her hips.

Smoothing a hand over his dark hair, she said, "Go find your brother and wash your hands. Dinner is almost ready."

"Okay."

As the kid dashed away, Kirsten motioned Brady inside. "Welcome to my world."

"Never a dull moment, huh?"

She closed the door behind him. "I wish."

"No, you don't." When she met his gaze, he added, "Just think how bored you'd be."

"They definitely keep me on my toes."

"They're four. That's their job." He eyed the inviting living room to his left with a blue-gray sofa near the wall and a matching chair and ottoman in front of the picture window opposite. A rustic side table holding a short stack of children's books was positioned between the oversized chair and a feminine wingback in muted shades of blue. "This looks great. And you've only been here, what, three days?"

"Yes. Don't give me too much credit, though. This is the only part of the house that's presentable. Everything else is still a work in progress."

"I understand. There are rooms at my place I still haven't touched. And I've been there three years."

"We done!" The twins raced into the room holding up, presumably, clean hands.

Kirsten glanced from them to Brady. "In that case, dinner is ready."

Following her into the kitchen, he silently prayed things between him and the boys would improve. As a deputy sheriff, Brady had tangled with people from all walks of life. Hardened criminals to high-ranking officials. Yet, their opinions had never mattered as much as those of these two boys.

Thankfully, Trevor's disappointment seemed to have waned as they gathered around the table. Though listening to two cheerful boys talk non-stop about horses, Daisy and, of course, dinosaurs, was kind of surreal. Brady couldn't believe how smart Jeremy and Trevor were. Not that he'd been around many four-year-olds. Still, this little glimpse into their world made him want to spend even more time with them.

"This soup is really good." He eyed Kirsten across the round wooden table that sat in front of the sliding doors, which opened to the backyard. She'd been kind of quiet since they sat down, making him wonder if she was having second thoughts about inviting him. Then again, he hadn't said much, either, what with Trevor and Jeremy doing most of the talking.

"Thank you. It's my mom's recipe." She dipped a piece of roll into her broth before popping it into her mouth.

He gathered another spoonful of meat and vegetables. "Your staff started today, correct?"

Nodding, she swallowed, dabbing her mouth with a napkin. "Things were pretty informal. Going over expectations, getting acquainted, discussing what comes next."

"Mr. Brady?"

Shifting his attention to his right, he addressed Jeremy. "Yes?"

"Do you want to see our dinosaurs?"

"We have *lots* of them." To Brady's left, an animated Trevor spread his arms wide.

It made Brady feel kind of special that they wanted to share something with him they were so enthusiastic about. "I sure would, but we need to finish our supper first."

"I'm done." Perching an elbow on the table, Trevor sighed, resting his chin in his hand.

Kirsten eyed his bowl, one brow lifting. "You didn't eat very much."

"I ate two rolls." He held up as many fingers.

His mother frowned. "Then perhaps you should make better choices next time, because you're not getting up from this table until you finish your soup."

The boy threw his head back and groaned as though he'd been sentenced to hard labor.

"It's good, Trevor. Look—" Jeremy pointed to his empty bowl "—mine's all gone." He sent a smile Kirsten's way. "'Cause I want a cookie."

"Aw," Trevor whined. "I forgot about the cookies we got at the store."

Brady caught Kirsten's gaze, wondering how she managed to remain strong. He'd have caved by now. "Plowman's cookies?" The farm supply store that was the closest thing to a grocery store in Hope Crossing also had one of the best bakeries around.

She nodded. "Chocolate chip."

"My favorite." Not to mention just about every

other variety. Looking at Trevor, he said, "We'd better finish so we can have one."

To his surprise, the boy straightened, his frown morphing into a grin. "I can beat you."

"Aw, no way," Brady teased, recalling that same competitive streak he'd once had.

"Uh-huh." Trevor picked up his spoon, his grin wide.

Soon, everyone's bowls were empty. Brady felt good that he'd played a small role in making that happen. He collected the dishes while Kirsten gave the boys their cookies.

He'd just placed the dishes and utensils in the sink beneath the window when she appeared beside him, holding the clear plastic container.

"Help yourself."

"Thank you." He snagged one, his gaze never leaving hers. "For everything. Supper was great and spending time with them—" he nodded in the direction of the chatterboxes still at the table "— well, this was the most enjoyable meal I've had in a very long time."

"You're welcome." Her big hazel eyes peered up at him. "And thank *you* for getting Trevor to eat." She sucked in a breath. "That boy likes to challenge me."

"Hmm. He must get that from you, because I would *never* do anything like that." Waggling his eyebrows, he took a big bite.

"Yeah, right." After claiming her own cookie,

she closed the container and set it on top of the refrigerator. "So tell me more about this barbecue bash."

Having polished off his cookie in short order, he said, "Sure. It's—"

"'S'cuse me."

At the repeated patting on his thigh, Brady lowered his gaze to find Jeremy craning his little neck to look up at him. He knelt to the boy's level. "Whatcha need, buddy?"

"Wanna come see our dinosaurs?"

Brady glanced up at Kirsten. "I sure do, but your mom and I—"

"That's all right," she said. "You go ahead. We can talk later."

He pushed to his feet, not wanting her to feel as though he were putting her off. "Are you sure?"

She reached for the faucet. "And miss an opportunity to clean the kitchen uninterrupted?"

That made him smile. "In that case, holler if you need me."

"Come on, Mr. Brady." Jeremy tugged his right hand. And when Trevor reached for his left, Brady felt as though he'd been redeemed.

Continuing into the living room, they led him across a blue, gray and white area rug to the fireplace at the far end of the space where dinosaurs of various shapes and sizes spread across the raised hearth.

"This is a Brachiosaurus." Jeremy held a miniature version of the long-necked creature.

"And 'dis is a Tyrannosaurus rex!" Standing atop the hearth, Trevor thrust a much larger creature baring its teeth toward Brady. "Roar!"

Recalling his long-ago affinity for the extinct reptiles, Brady said, "Do you have a Stegosaurus?"

"Yes." Jeremy quickly located one and held it up.

Rubbing the stubble on his chin, Brady probed the recesses of his mind. "How about an Ankylosaurus?"

"Right here." Trevor held it up.

Brady grinned. "You fellas are pretty smart."

Cocking his little head, Jeremy peered up at him. "Do you have dinosaurs?"

"I used to." His mother had even bought him a book on the prehistoric creatures and would sit and read it to him for hours. Well, what had seemed like hours to a five-year-old, anyway. He recalled the fascination in her voice. And the fragrance of her rose perfume.

Humph. Where had that come from?

He eased to the floor, listening to the boys go on and on about their favorite creatures. Until he noticed Kirsten watching them from the opposite side of the room, her head tilted slightly. What was she thinking?

"Come see our room." Again, Trevor pulled at his hand.

Fearing that might make Kirsten uncomfortable, Brady said, "Maybe next time." He pushed to his feet. "I need to talk to your mama for a bit now."

The boy looked toward his mother. "Can we watch a show?"

"A short one." Kirsten retrieved a remote from the television stand situated along the wall opposite the fireplace. "Then it'll be time to get ready for bed."

The boys parked on the sofa, groaning until the cartoon began to play.

Brady then followed Kirsten into the kitchen, curiosity getting the best of him. "I saw you watching me and the boys. What was going through your head?"

Her deep breath told him she was choosing her words carefully. "The boys look so much like you. Even your mannerisms are similar. The way you and Trevor both stood with your hands on your hips." She finally met his gaze. "Brady, when people see you with us—with them—aren't you afraid that could impact your campaign for sheriff?"

He watched her for a moment. Was she looking for an excuse to create some distance between him and his sons? Or was she genuinely worried?

He'd give her the benefit of the doubt. "No. But I appreciate your concern. And thank you again for inviting me. Tonight has been incredible. I never imagined I could feel this way." He rubbed the back of his neck, trying to grasp the flurry of emotions building inside of him. "I mean, I just met them and yet I have this all-consuming desire to be with them and know everything about them."

She leaned her backside against the counter, her expression softening. "You love them."

The words stopped him in his tracks. "Yeah. I guess I do. How can that be when I just met them, though?"

"I can't explain it." She shrugged. "But I get it. I fell in love with them the first time I heard their hearts beating and saw them moving on the sonogram."

"I wish I could've been there." He cringed as soon as the words left his mouth. "I'm sorry. That wasn't meant as a jab. I just—" Sighing, he shook his head. "I've missed so much. And I'm not trying to cast blame on you. I should have told you why I didn't want children. Looking back on that day we broke up, I wish I'd handled things differently. That I'd told you about the Huntington's. But I was afraid."

"Of what?"

He lifted a shoulder. "That you'd feel stuck. That even if you wanted to step away, you'd stay with me out of pity."

Shaking her head, she puffed out a laugh.

"What's so funny?"

"What you just said." Her gaze finally met his. "I didn't tell you I was pregnant for that same reason."

He chuckled. "Sounds like we're both adept at fooling ourselves."

"I guess so."

And he couldn't help wondering how different their lives might have been if they'd simply been honest with one another.

Between watching Brady with Jeremy and Trevor, not to mention all the woulda, coulda, shouldas brought on by her conversation with him, Kirsten found it difficult to sleep. Telling Brady about the boys had changed everything. And she couldn't help wondering how it would impact their lives going forward.

Thankfully, she had plenty to distract her at the urgent care center Thursday. She and her staff had spent hours unpacking, sorting and putting away everything from exam lights and sharps containers to swabs, thermometers and bandages in preparation for their inspection tomorrow. And thanks to some great teamwork, they finished before five o'clock. Now all Kirsten wanted was a quiet evening with her boys.

All right, so quiet was relative with Jeremy and Trevor, but she'd settle for snuggling on the couch and watching a movie. Anything to distract her from recalling how great Brady was with the twins or how he seemed to regret the choices he'd made in the past.

"We knocked it out, ladies." Wearing blue scrubs because they were the only thing she could find that were clean this morning, Kirsten grabbed three water bottles from the refrigerator in the tiny staff lounge, which also had a small table and chairs, as well as a coffee maker and microwave that were perched atop the counter alongside the sink. "I appreciate all of your hard work." She handed one bottle to Dawn, a fifty-something registered nurse who'd traded her job at a physician's office in Brenham to work closer to home, and the other to Kara, her office manager and married mother of two, who also lived locally.

"You are so welcome." Dawn had a contagious smile. "The people of Hope Crossing have been praying long and hard for access to basic health care right here in town."

Kara nodded her agreement. "Folks can hardly wait for us to open."

Their words bolstered Kirsten, giving her hope for these first six months. "That's good to hear." Twisting the cap on her drink, she added, "Meeting the health care needs of the community is what we're all about."

After a little more chitchat, they gathered their personal belongings and started toward the reception area, turning off lights as they went.

Kirsten was digging her keys out of her back-pack when Dawn said, "Well, would you lookie there. Hope Crossing's favorite deputy."

Deputy? Kirsten jerked her head toward the front door. What was Brady doing here?

Dawn pushed open the door. "Hey, Brady. What brings you by?"

"Hello, Dawn." He stepped inside, his smile wide. "Kara." He nodded. "I just stopped in to talk to Kirsten."

A smile tugged at the corners of Dawn's mouth, her eyebrows lifting. "And...how do you two know each other?"

"My brother, Scott, and Brady were army buddies." Kirsten approached, eager to squash any romantic notions the other women might entertain.

Brady nodded. "Scott was a good man."

"Was?" Dawn cocked her head.

"He was killed in a training accident several years ago," said Brady.

The older woman frowned. "I'm sorry to hear that."

"How sad." Kara slid her purse strap over her shoulder.

"Scott made me promise that if anything ever happened to him, I'd look after Kirsten." His gaze darted her way before returning to Dawn.

Kirsten's chest tightened, her gaze narrowing. Was that all she'd been to Brady? An obligation?

"You're a good man, Brady. We could use a lot

more like you." Dawn patted him on the shoulder as she started for the door. "Kirsten, I'll see you in the morning, hon."

Kara followed Dawn with a wave. "See ya tomorrow."

Brady stared at the floor as the door closed. "I'm a horrible person." When he lifted his gaze, Kirsten saw pain in his eyes that hadn't been there before. "I made Scott a promise. Yet instead of following through, I turned my back on you when you needed me most."

Her breath caught in her throat. She looked away, not wanting to see the regret in his eyes. "I'm a big girl. I can take care of myself."

"I like to think I'm a man of my word."

She lifted her chin, forcing herself to look at him. "I am *not* your responsibility, Brady."

"You're the mother of my children."

"And I've done just fine without you." His wince indicated her barb had hit its mark.

He cocked his head, those ocean eyes never leaving hers. "If you hadn't come to Hope Crossing, you never would've told me about Jeremy and Trevor, would you?"

She swallowed around the sudden lump in her throat. How many times had she contemplated telling him? Yet, each time she'd talked herself out of it, convinced it wouldn't make any difference because he didn't want children. "I don't—"

"Oh, come on. You said it yourself that first day

you came to the house. That you only told me so I wouldn't be blindsided."

Yes, she had. "Seems we've both made our share of mistakes."

Nodding, he rubbed the back of his neck and stared at the floor.

Eager to move past the awkwardness, she sighed. "I'm assuming that's not the conversation you were expecting when you came in here."

Snorting, he lowered his hand. "Not even close." His gaze met hers. "Actually, there were two things."

She lifted a brow, waiting.

"I scheduled an appointment to begin the testing process. It's two weeks from yesterday."

"Oh. That's good." Her smile felt weak. "Thank you."

"And since we didn't get to discuss the Boot Scoot'n Barbecue Bash last night, I thought I'd ask you and the twins to join *me* for supper."

She stared up at him, blinking. "Tonight?"

"Yeah."

Spending another evening with Brady was the last thing she wanted. Especially after what just transpired. The only thing worse would be spending a guilt-ridden evening at home. Oh, why had she offered to help him?

"I'm serving lasagna, Caesar salad and garlic bread."

"That's rather ambitious." Not to mention unfair. He knew how much she loved Italian.

"Nah. The bread and lasagna are frozen, though delicious nonetheless."

Unable to say no, she found herself pulling into Brady's driveway an hour later with two enthusiastic little boys in the back seat.

"Maybe we can ride da horses." The glee in Trevor's voice had Kirsten ready to turn around and go back home.

"But it's getting dark," Jeremy reasoned. "We can't ride the horseys in the dark."

Eyeing them in her rearview mirror, she couldn't help smiling. Her boys were her world. A world that was suddenly shifting. And she was finding it difficult to keep her equilibrium.

By the time she opened the back door for the twins, they had unbuckled from their booster seats.

Jeremy eased out first. "Daisy," he cheered as his feet hit the gravel drive.

Despite the rapidly waning daylight, Kirsten could see the pale yellow dog trotting toward them, tail wagging, while her master trailed behind.

Wearing faded jeans and a gray pullover with the sleeves pushed up, Brady smiled as he approached. "Hey, gang."

Trevor hopped out and peered up at Brady. "Can we ride your horse?"

His smile unwavering, Brady shook his head. "Sorry, fellas. No rides tonight. Though I could use some help feeding my horses."

While the boys cheered, Kirsten's body went rigid. She glared at Brady. He hadn't mentioned anything about horses, feeding or otherwise. If he had, she would've not only voiced her displeasure, but also used the opportunity to set a few ground rules. Then again, perhaps that was why he hadn't said anything.

Before she could object, though, he started up the drive, a boy on either side of him.

Watching them go, she tossed the door closed with a little too much force.

Amid the mild evening air, Daisy nudged Kirsten's other hand with her wet nose.

She petted the sweet dog who'd probably never met a stranger. "Yeah, you like me now, but how will you feel when I wring your master's neck?"

Nearing Brady and the boys at the side of the house, she slowed her steps, purposely lagging behind so she could hear their conversation. The banter between the three males made her heart squeeze. This was what she'd dreamed of. For Jeremy and Trevor to have the opportunity to build a relationship with their father.

Yet while Brady seemed just as smitten with them, how would he feel once the newness wore off? When the boys challenged him? Or they were sick? When they no longer thought he was the coolest thing since dinosaurs?

Was Brady ready to go the distance? He certainly hadn't been with her.

And he acknowledged his mistake.

Yes, but she didn't want any mistakes where Jeremy and Trevor were concerned.

The guys' chatter continued as Brady led them into the backyard. Lights glowed from the back of the farmhouse, as well as the red-metal barn across the way. And as the boys' excitement grew, she moved alongside them.

"Boys, Daisy would like some attention. Can you play with her while I talk to Mr. Brady?"

Jeremy turned. "Aww, poor Daisy."

Patting his denim-covered legs, Trevor said, "C'mere, girl."

While the canine rushed the boys, Kirsten stepped several feet away, motioning for Brady to follow.

"What's up?"

Drawing her cardigan around her, she lowered her voice. "You didn't say anything about feeding your horses."

He looked perplexed. "It's what I always do before supper. I got delayed, though, because I had to get the lasagna in the oven."

"I understand." She crossed her arms. "But the boys have never been around horses before, so we need some ground rules."

He stared down at her, his hands settling on his hips. "Such as?"

"I do *not* want them riding or even sitting atop a horse."

One dark brow lifted. "We're only feeding them." Cocking his head slightly, he added, "But you know they're going to want to do both of those things at some point."

"Which is why we're discussing it now."

He studied her for a moment. "What else?"

"I guess that's it." For now. "Basically, I don't want them doing anything that could put them at risk."

"What risk?" His brow furrowed. "Do you really think I'd put them in danger?"

Lifting her chin, she said, "Not on purpose. Though I'm certain our definitions of dangerous are quite different."

"Says the woman who parasailed over the Pacific and swam in shark-infested waters."

"We were in a cage." She glanced around him to make sure the boys were still distracted with Daisy. "The sharks couldn't get to us." Looking up at him again, she added, "Besides, that was BC."

"BC?"

"Before children."

He glared down at her. "You know, there's such a thing as overprotective."

"Not when it comes to four-year-old twins."

He stepped closer, his nostrils flaring. "Kirsten,

you might have more parenting experience than I do, but it's not like I lack common sense. When it comes to horses, I know exactly what I'm doing. And the more those boys know, the safer they'll be."

She took a step back. "All right, then. So long as we're on the same page."

He stared at her, drawing in a deep breath before turning back to the boys. "Who's ready to feed some horses?"

Little hands shot into the air, along with collective cries of "Me!"

As they all continued through the gate and toward the barn, Kirsten breathed a sigh of relief. But what if she hadn't been here to question Brady? To make sure he understood her expectations.

Inhaling the crisp evening air, she realized there was only one thing she could do going forward. Whenever the boys were with Brady, she had to be there, too. No matter how many times her traitorous heart threatened to turn on her.

Chapter Five

Brady wasn't used to being called out. Yet while having Kirsten treat him like he was an impulsive teenager was annoying, he knew it stemmed from her fierce love for their sons. Sooner or later, though, she'd have to loosen her hold on the reins and learn to trust him. Though he may have an uphill battle.

Still, learning about horses started with the basics. So as they neared the barn, he stopped and knelt to the boys' level. Something he would've done even if Kirsten hadn't lectured him. "A couple of rules, guys. First, no running in the barn. Second, we use our inside voices. We don't want to scare the horses."

"Okay." The boys nodded, their blue eyes wide with anticipation.

Standing, he reached for the door at one end of the building and slid it open, light spilling outside as he gestured toward Kirsten. "Ladies first."

She tentatively moved inside, motioning for the

boys to follow her. As if they needed the encouragement.

Brady joined them as one of the horses nickered.

Jeremy and Trevor gasped, their eyes growing wide as they gazed down the center aisle to find each of the five horses poking their curious heads over the stall doors to stare straight at them.

"Whoa," the boys said collectively.

They were about to start toward the horses when their mother set a hand atop each of their shoulders. "Wait for Mr. Brady."

"It appears the gang's all here." Brady opened the door to the tack room. "We'd best get to work, fellas."

"Yeah." The boys rushed to help him.

While Daisy supervised, Brady scooped feed from the bins, then let Jeremy and Trevor take turns dumping it into the buckets labeled with each horse's name.

Noting Kirsten hadn't joined them, Brady dared a glance over his shoulder and found her standing in the doorway, arms crossed, her gaze laser focused on him and the boys.

"What is 'dis stuff?" Trevor scrunched his nose.

"Horse feed." Brady picked up a few pellets. "These have all sorts of vitamins and minerals the horses need to stay healthy."

The curious duo continued to pepper him with questions, though Brady didn't mind. Horses were his passion. One he intended to share with them the way his parents had done with him.

After adding supplements and treats to the buckets, Brady stacked them together. "All right, fellas, we are ready to feed."

When they approached the first stall, Brady said, "Boys, this here is Nutmeg." He'd taken in the sweet filly after her owners could no longer afford to keep her.

The boys had their heads tilted all the way back to peer up at the creature eyeing them over the four-foot wooden partition.

Realizing they were at a disadvantage, Brady set the buckets on the floor and crossed the aisle to the open space opposite the tack room where he stored hay and other items. "Let's see if we can't give you fellas a better view." He grabbed a folding step stool, then returned to position it beside the stall. "Hop on up there."

While the boys gleefully climbed the two steps that allowed them to see over the half wall, Brady couldn't help noticing Kirsten's glare darting between him, the boys and Nutmeg. And once the boys were atop the stool, she moved behind them.

Choosing not to say anything, Brady slid the gate open and stepped inside the stall.

"Hi, Nutmeg." The twins' smiles were wide as they reached their hands toward the animal. The filly ignored them, though. She was only interested in what was in the bucket.

"Boys…" Warning laced Kirsten's tone. "Keep your hands to yourselves unless Mr. Brady says it's okay."

"This gal only wants to eat right now." He emptied the contents of her bucket into her feeder. Then, while Nutmeg went to work sorting out the treats, he topped off her water bucket in the corner.

Closing the gate behind him moments later, he said, "All right, that's one down, four more to go."

While he'd feared the boys might lose interest, they were as enthralled with every other horse as they had been with Nutmeg. And they were even more excited when Digger let them pet him.

After the food and water were dispensed, Brady filled the hay nets in each stall.

"That didn't take as long as I thought it would." Kirsten shoved her hands in the pockets of her sweater when they exited the barn. "Though I'm sure it's even quicker when you don't have any— shall we say—assistants."

He eyed the rising moon, wondering if she was hoping he wouldn't want the boys helping him again. "Just a few minutes. No big deal." He rubbed a hand over his stomach. "I don't know about the rest of you, but I'm ready for supper. That lasagna should be ready soon." His whole house probably smelled amazing.

Yet when they stepped into the kitchen, there were no enticing aromas of garlic, tomato sauce and melted cheese. Instead, the space smelled the same as it had when he left.

He crossed to the stove, his hopes of impressing Kirsten decreasing with each step. Opening the oven, he peered inside, groaning at the sight of a still frozen casserole.

"Problem?" Kirsten asked somewhere behind him.

He glanced at the controls. "I forgot to turn on the oven." He removed the pan and set it atop the stove, distinctly recalling setting the temperature. He must not have hit the Start button.

What were they going to eat now? Two little boys wouldn't be happy with salad and bread.

When he heard Kirsten stifle a laugh behind him, he could only imagine what she was thinking. That he was inept. That she couldn't wait to get the boys out of there.

Turning, he said, "I'm glad you think this is funny."

She promptly sobered. Though her lips continued to twitch. "Only because I've done the same thing."

"What did you do?"

"What any mom desperate to get dinner on the table would do. I took to the internet to find out how to cook it in the microwave." She smiled. "Would you like me to show you?"

A short time later, while the boys explored his old marble collection at the table, Kirsten watched him prepare the salad. "Shall we discuss the Boot Scoot'n Barbecue thing?"

He added croutons and shredded parmesan to the bagged romaine he'd already emptied into a bowl. "I don't know much since this is the first time we've done anything like this. Near as I can tell, though, they want both the kids and adults to enjoy themselves." Snagging a cup towel from the counter, he wiped his hands as he faced her. "I mean, adults are fine with eatin' and talkin', but kids like to be entertained."

"Indoor or outdoor event?"

"Indoor, which, I think, is a bigger challenge. If it was going to be warm outside, I'd say get a big ol' bounce house and call it good. But who knows what the weather will be like in February."

"Could be ice or sweltering heat." She leaned against the counter. "So we need something that can be done inside. Something that makes the kids feel like they're part of the event instead of tagging along with their parents."

"Exactly." He grabbed the garlic bread from the freezer and set it aside before retrieving a sheet pan from the cupboard.

"One thing the boys and their friends always seemed to gravitate to is face painting, but we'd need someone—two or three someones, actually—who would be willing to do that. I don't suppose you know any teenagers, do you?"

He lifted a shoulder. "A few from church. Gloriana Broussard—the one who tasked me with this—has a sixteen-year-old daughter. Maybe she and a couple of her friends would be willing to help. Though I'm not exactly sold on the face paintings."

"Okay, then what about some interactive activities or crafts? Maybe we could take their pictures and they could decorate frames to display them in. But we'd need a printer, so that might not be feasible."

Removing the bread from the packaging, he pried the loaf in two and laid each half on the pan. "Wouldn't frames be kind of pricey?" Opening the preheated oven, he placed the pan inside, closed the door and set the timer before facing her.

"Not if they're made out of tongue depressors."

The corners of his mouth lifted. "What'll they decorate them with? Cotton balls and swabs?"

"You're hilarious, James." Her comment along with the look she sent him reminded him of the playful banter they'd once shared on a regular basis. He'd missed that. Missed her.

Save for his horses, his life was rather boring. He glanced toward the table. Now he was a father. Just knowing that brought new meaning to his life. Something he hadn't realized was missing. Something that would be a driving force in everything he did from now on. And that was both terrifying and exciting.

* * *

Despite the clinic passing inspection on Friday and getting her house put to rights yesterday, Kirsten's stomach churned as she pulled into the sparsely filled parking lot of Hope Crossing Bible Church Sunday morning. All she had to do now was get the boys inside and to their classroom before Brady showed up. Because once people saw them all together, it was only a matter of time before they became curious. So for the sake of Brady's campaign, she wanted to postpone the inevitable as long as possible.

Retrieving her Bible and purse from the passenger seat, she eyed the boys in the rearview mirror. "Are you two ready to make some new friends?"

"Yay," they cheered. Though Trevor was more outgoing than Jeremy, the fact that they always had each other seemed to bolster their confidence when visiting new places.

Wearing a casual sage-green dress with a tiered skirt over a pair of boots, she gathered her things and emerged from her SUV into the cool morning air, the brilliant blue sky hinting at a beautiful day. She slipped her purse over her shoulder and closed the door before reaching for the back door. Before she opened it, though, the sound of an approaching vehicle gave her pause.

She glanced to her right, her chest tightening when she spotted Brady's truck aiming for the parking spot next to hers. Evidently, he hadn't gotten the hint when she'd declined last night's invitation to ride together. Could he not foresee a problem with the four of them being seen together?

Hugging her Bible against her chest, she watched as he eased to a stop beside her. Moments later, he exited to round the front of his truck, his smile wide.

The hairs on her arms raised. Good gracious, he looked fine. Between the dark wash jeans, Sunday-go-to-meeting boots and the medium-gray pearl-snap shirt that made his blue eyes even bluer, she was feeling a little unsteady. And that was wrong on so many levels.

"You're here early." He seemed clueless that had been her plan. One he'd now upended.

"I wanted to give myself plenty of time to get the boys situated in their classroom." Brady had told her they had childcare for preschoolers.

"I'm glad I came early then so I can help you find your way around."

"Oh, you don't—" She paused as another vehicle seemed to capture his attention. Following his gaze, she saw a graphite-colored pickup truck approach. And the driver was obviously someone Brady knew.

As the vehicle came to a stop on the other side of hers, Brady said, "That would be my dad."

Peering down at her, he added, "He's been looking forward to meeting the boys."

Her grip tightened around her Bible. Brady had the same dark hair and blue eyes as his father. And the twins favored Brady.

A ruckus from inside her vehicle had her gaze drifting to the window to discover the boys unbuckled and eagerly waiting for her to open the door.

With a deep breath and a prayer for strength, she did just that.

After leaping onto the pavement clad in khaki jeans and Henley shirts in their respective blue and red, the boys peppered Brady with questions as though it had been ages since they'd seen him instead of just last night. He'd come by her place after he got off duty, bearing carryout pizza he'd picked up along the way so she wouldn't have to cook. Then he'd entertained the boys while she did laundry and he'd helped her hang the last of her pictures.

While the boys continued to chatter, Hank appeared at the back of her vehicle, his smile widening when he spotted the grandsons he had yet to meet.

In that moment, Kirsten's heart pinched. Because while Brady might have been adamant about not wanting children, his father likely didn't feel the same way. Yet, she'd prevented Hank from knowing his grandsons.

His gaze drifted to hers and she swallowed hard. Would he hate her for keeping the boys a secret?

Instead, his smile never wavered, and he sent her a wink. "Looks like you've got some new friends, Brady."

Both boys looked up at the older gentleman.

"Who are you?" Trevor's bluntness had her cringing.

"This is my dad." Brady looked from the boys to his father. "Dad, this is Jeremy—" he motioned to the boy in blue "—and his brother, Trevor."

She was impressed he was able to tell them apart. Or maybe he was on to her color coding. Something she did regularly so others wouldn't get the boys confused.

Hank knelt to the boys' level the way Brady so often did and extended a hand. "Pleased to meet you, fellas."

Jeremy took hold first. "What's your name, Mr. Brady's dad?"

The older man chuckled. "That is a bit of a mouthful. How 'bout you fellas call me Mr. Hank?" He let go of Jeremy's hand as the boys looked at each other, seemingly assessing his offer.

"Okay, Mr. Hank." Trevor shook the man's hand.

When he pushed to his feet moments later, Hank moved around Brady to Kirsten and gave her a side hug. "Good to see you again, young lady."

Reciprocating the surprising gesture, she said, "You, too, Hank."

By now, a steady stream of vehicles poured into the parking lot.

"Looks like we'd best get a move on," said Hank.

Kirsten shifted her Bible to her left arm, then held out her right hand to Trevor only to see him reach for Brady's. Her gaze drifted to Jeremy who was watching Hank.

"Mama says we're s'posed to hold hands when there's cars," the boy said.

Hank smiled. "Your mama is very wise." He sent her a wink as Jeremy placed his small hand into Hank's large one.

And just like that, her carefully crafted plan to protect Brady's reputation had been blown to smithereens.

Once they were inside the steepled beige-brick building, Hank headed for the sanctuary, promising to save her and Brady a seat while Brady accompanied her and the boys to the nursery.

"Good morning, Dottie." Brady said as they approached the half door of the colorful room that was decorated in a Noah's ark theme.

"Mornin', Brady." The woman's brow puckered. "We don't usually see you 'round here. What can I do for you?"

"I'd like you to meet my friend Kirsten and her twin boys, Jeremy and Trevor."

"Oh, my." Grinning, Dottie looked from Kirsten to the boys. "What handsome young men. How old are you?"

They each held up four fingers, though Jeremy leaned against Kirsten's leg, suddenly shy.

"Well, I'm so glad you came to visit me." Dottie opened the door and motioned for the boys to enter, her gaze moving from them to Kirsten and Brady before darting back to the twins.

Kirsten's stomach knotted. Had Dottie noticed the resemblance?

"Jeremy is in the blue," Brady offered. "And Trevor is in red."

Kirsten cringed. She should have been the one to tell Dottie that, not him. Didn't he realize he was only fueling an impending inferno?

"'Preciate the tip, Brady." Dottie winked Kirsten's way, closing the door. "You two enjoy the service." With a final wave, she turned her attention to the twins. "Are you boys ready to have some fun?"

Brady urged Kirsten away from the door. "Don't worry, Dottie's been doing this for a long time. The boys are in good hands."

Was he really that obtuse? It wasn't the boys she was worried about. Yet, she seemed to be the only person who was concerned. Neither Brady nor his dad were bothered, so why should she stress over it? She had plenty of other things to worry about. Such as making sure the urgent care center proved successful.

"So, I was thinking," Brady continued as they strode down the long hallway that led back to the sanctuary. "Maybe you and the boys could come over this afternoon so they can try out some of the toys I told you about." Last night he'd informed her he'd done some online shopping and purchased a whole host of items he couldn't wait for the boys to try out.

Still, it meant spending even more time with him. She supposed she'd better get used to it, though. She wasn't ready to leave the three of them alone just yet. Not with all those horses.

"Sure. Maybe after lunch."

"Brady, just the person I was hoping to see."

Kirsten looked up to find a beautiful woman with long dark hair and a baby on her hip approaching them.

"Gloriana." The way Brady tensed suggested there was a history between him and this woman.

"At ease, soldier." Smiling, the woman stopped in front of him, her gaze drifting to Kirsten. "Hello there." She extended her free hand. "I'm Gloriana Broussard."

"Kirsten Reynolds." She accepted the gesture. "Who's this little guy?" She couldn't help smiling at the drooling baby boy she guessed to be about five or six months old.

"This is Benjamin, who is teething and not all that happy about it."

"Aw, I can't say that I blame him." Kirsten smoothed a hand over the infant's dark downy hair. "Have you tried a chilled teething ring or rubbing his gums?"

"Not only is Kirsten the mother of twins, she's a nurse practitioner," Brady said.

Gloriana's eyes widened. "Oh, so you know all about this. Yes to the rubbing. I'll have to try the teething ring. Do I put it in the freezer?"

"Refrigerator is fine. Worst case, you can give him some over-the-counter pain reliever." Watching the child gum his mama's finger, she added, "Though he seems to be content now."

Brady cleared his throat. "You said you wanted to see me."

Gloriana jerked her head up. "Yes, to let you know that I spoke to Kyleigh and her friend Callie, and they'd be happy to help in whatever capacity you need at the bash." She looked at Kirsten again. "Wait, are you the friend who's helping him brainstorm ideas?"

"Guilty." Kirsten shrugged. "Not that I've been much help."

"Between the two of you, I'm sure you'll come up with something amazing." Adjusting little Benjamin, Gloriana said, "I'd best get this fella to the nursery. Nice to meet you, Kirsten."

"Likewise."

Kirsten felt a little lighter as she and Brady continued toward the sanctuary. "Gloriana seems very nice."

"I s'pose." Though his body language said otherwise.

"Do the two of you have some sort of history?" She immediately regretted asking. Or, perhaps, it was the sudden twinge in the vicinity of her heart that had her on edge. Was Gloriana an old girlfriend?

Hands in his pockets, he nodded at someone as they passed. "Yes, but not like you're thinking."

"And what am I thinking?"

"We never dated."

"But I'm guessing you wanted to."

Approaching the sanctuary, he said, "I really don't want to talk about this right now."

While he got points for being honest, her curiosity had been piqued.

As promised, Hank had saved them seats in the modest sanctuary with sand-colored carpet, matching cushioned wood pews and beautiful stained-glass windows. And soon enough, she was sitting between the two James men. Something that didn't feel quite as awkward as she would have expected.

"Did the boys do okay?" Hank asked as she sat down.

"Yes, they did. Thank you."

He leaned slightly, bringing Brady into the conversation. "What would y'all think about joining me for lunch after church? I thought we could head on over to Brenham for some Mexican food. My treat."

Kirsten had been prepared to weasel her way out of the man's invitation until he'd suggested Mexican. She'd been craving enchiladas all week. Back in College Station, she frequented her favorite Tex-Mex place every chance she got. But that wasn't an option in Hope Crossing.

"Sounds good to me." Brady looked at her as the piano began to play. "What do you say, Kirsten?"

That meant spending even more time with Brady. But then, she hated to deprive Hank of the opportunity to visit with the boys when he seemed so enthralled with them. Especially since he'd been so kind despite her having kept the twins a secret.

That alone left her with little choice. "Sounds good to me, too."

Chapter Six

Kirsten had not planned to spend her entire Sunday with Brady. Yes, she had agreed to bring the boys to his place this afternoon, but that was before Hank invited them all to lunch. When she hesitated, Brady then offered to take the boys home with him and give her a break, but she wasn't ready to release that much control. Not when the boys were so infatuated with his horses.

So, after lunch, she and the boys had returned home long enough to change clothes before going to Brady's. Her only consolation was the sunny sixty-eight degrees that made her want to be outside.

When Brady had told her he'd done some shopping, he wasn't kidding. He had games, race cars, walkie-talkies and, of course, dinosaurs. Though she suspected the three-pack of lightsabers were more for Brady than the boys. He'd always been a big *Star Wars* fan.

Right now, he and the boys were playing with their new T-ball set in his backyard while she soaked in some vitamin D. Brady was pretty proud of the miniature ball diamond he'd set up. And she was thrilled with anything that kept the boys away from the horses. While she had grown somewhat comfortable with them helping Brady feed the animals, that was as far as she was willing to go. Despite Brady's insistence they learn the basics of riding. Jeremy and Trevor were too young and horses were too unpredictable. Having lost both her dad and Scott, she preferred to play it safe.

For now, she was content to sit on the porch steps and take in the scene that, until today, had only lived in her dreams. Jeremy and Trevor playing with their father while she applauded their hits, groaned over their misses and encouraged them to try again. She'd even taken some video and sent it to her mother who'd responded with lots of hearts.

"I could use a snack." Brady looked over at the boys. "How 'bout you?"

"Yeah," they said in unison.

Brady eyed her as he started up the steps. "Care to join us? Don't tell the boys, but I've got some chocolate chip cookies stashed away."

She held up a hand. "Nothing for me. I'm still bloated from lunch. I can help you, though." Pushing to her feet, she looked at the boys on lawn. "Y'all throw Daisy her ball for a bit. I think she feels left out."

Inside Brady's rustic yet quaint kitchen, she saw

him reach into the refrigerator. When he emerged, he was holding some string-cheese packets and four small water bottles.

"Let me help you." She hurried to relieve him of the bottles.

"Thanks." Closing the door with his elbow, he said, "I thought I'd offer some healthier options, too."

She couldn't help smiling. "You're thinking like a parent now. The boys actually love string cheese."

He set the items on the counter, his smile instantaneous. "That's good to know. I got some of those fruit snacks, too." He started toward the pantry.

"You know those aren't really healthy, right?"

Retrieving the box, he shrugged. "Yeah, but they're in the shapes of those cartoon characters they like." He showed her the puppy images.

Something as simple as fruit snacks should not warm her heart so much. But Brady's desire to be involved in her boys'—his sons'—lives and make them happy was hitting all the right notes.

Clearing her throat, she watched as he added them to the other items before opening the cupboard. "So, what's the story with you and Gloriana?" Hearing the words had her cringing. While she'd merely been looking for a distraction, Brady probably thought she'd been dwelling on that all day.

He pulled out a plastic bowl, set it on the counter and began adding the items to it. "Gloriana's the reason I spent my senior year at a military school."

Kirsten felt her eyes widen. "How did she do that?"

His cheeks grew red as he admitted having a teenage crush on Gloriana, and how she'd used him in a retaliation campaign against one of their teachers.

"Brady, that was a long time ago."

"I know, but it still sticks in my craw that she never defended—"

"Mama! Mama!" Jeremy yelled from outside.

Kirsten's gaze collided with Brady's before they rushed out the door to find Jeremy racing across the yard, his face red. But where was Trevor?

Hurrying down the steps, she said, "What is it?"

"Trevor!" Jeremy pointed toward the barn. "He tried to get the horsey and he fell into the horsey stall."

"The horses should be in the pasture," said Brady.

Jeremy shook his head. "We sawed Chief go in da barn."

Brady's eyes widened before he sprinted across the yard.

That had Kirsten grabbing Jeremy and running as fast as she could with an almost-forty-pound weight on her hip.

By the time she reached the barn, Brady was emerging from a stall at the far end, cradling Trevor in his arms, Daisy staring up at them.

Kirsten's heart dropped. Was Trevor hurt? Or worse?

Swallowing around the lump in her throat, she stood Jeremy on the rubber mat covering the concrete, took hold of his hand and marched that way.

"I only wanted to pet Chief," Trevor sobbed as Brady laid him on the floor and knelt beside him, appearing to examine him.

Kirsten dropped next to them. "You boys know you're not supposed to be in here without an adult." Her gaze roamed over Trevor, looking for any cuts or bruises. She felt his head, checking for swelling. "Do you hurt anywhere?" As he shook his head, she noticed a slight abrasion on his chin.

"He seemed pretty shaken when I found him on the floor." Brady looked from his son to her. "My guess is he got the wind knocked out of him."

And as Trevor's tears subsided, she concurred with Brady's assessment.

A few minutes later, Trevor sat up, swiping tears with his sleeve.

Thank You for protecting him, Lord!

Looking from Trevor to Jeremy, she said, "What compelled you two to come in here, anyway?"

"We sawed Chief go in the barn, and we wanted to say hi," Jeremy said.

"But how did you—?" Glancing toward the

stall, Kirsten noticed the stepladder pushed up against it. The one Brady let the boys stand on so they could see the horses when he fed them. "How did that get there?"

The boys shared sheepish expressions.

"It was the only way we could see the horsey." Jeremy set his little hand on her shoulder. "We sorry, Mama."

Standing, Kirsten hugged herself, willing her shaking to stop. Her heart thundered in her chest. "Boys, I want you to take Daisy outside, please."

While Jeremy eagerly coaxed the dog to follow him, Trevor dragged his feet, his head hung low.

When they were finally out of sight, Kirsten turned her attention to Brady. "I was afraid something like this would happen."

Brady's cheeks reddened, his gaze narrowing. "It wouldn't have happened if you'd've allowed me to give them some instruction."

Her fists balled at her sides. "Oh, so this is my fault?"

He gestured toward the front of the barn. "They're curious. The best way to overcome that is with knowledge. You can't protect them from everything, Kirsten."

"Funny, I never had a problem before."

"Yeah? Well, I'm not the one who left them alone in the backyard."

A gasp lodged in her throat. Her hand flew to her mouth. He was right. He said he'd get the snacks, yet she'd followed him, leaving the twins unattended.

Turning away, she fought to hold herself together. She'd allowed herself to become distracted. How could she have done that?

Tears spilled onto her cheeks. She squeezed her eyes shut, willing no more to fall.

"I'm sorry, Kirsten." She could feel Brady in front of her now, his voice low and calm as his palms cupped her elbows. "I shouldn't have said that."

She hauled in a sloppy sob-riddled breath. "It's true, though."

His arms came around her and she breathed in his familiar essence, realizing how much she'd missed it. Missed him and the strength he offered.

"Then I should've mentioned it earlier. Instead, I weaponized it."

Peering up at him through watery eyes, she said, "I love them so much. I'm terrified of losing them like my dad and Scott." *And you.*

Brady smoothed a hand over her hair, his penetrating gaze tearing down her defenses. "I will do everything in my power to prevent that from happening. But you have to trust me. Let me teach them horsemanship, the way my parents taught me. Please, Kirsten?"

"What will that look like, though?"

Lowering his hands, he took a step back and she chastised herself for missing the comfort of his embrace. "It means teaching them the basics. Having them ride with us."

"I haven't ridden in ages." The last time had been at his father's place when she and Brady were dating. She'd always enjoyed it, though. Found it relaxing. Or was that simply because she'd been with Brady?

"I've seen you in the saddle. Once you're in it again, you'll know exactly what to do."

"Aren't horses unpredictable, though?"

"Only if they feel threatened. I would never put you or the boys on a horse I wasn't certain about."

The boys' giggles carried on the breeze and into the barn causing Brady to smile.

"Sounds like they're no worse for the wear."

Shaking her head, she puffed out a laugh. "Meanwhile, they shaved ten years off of my life." She looked up at Brady. "I know how much you love horses, so it's understandable you'd want to share that with Jeremy and Trevor." She drew in a shaky breath. "So yes, I will allow you to teach them. But please keep in mind that their mama isn't near as confident as you are."

"I promise." He glanced toward the open door at the opposite end of the barn. "I'd better check on them. If you need a few minutes, though, I understand."

"I appreciate that."

As he strode away, she turned her attention to the brown horse with a black mane that had been at the center of this afternoon's drama. Chief munched on hay, seemingly oblivious to what had transpired.

"Thank you for not hurting my son."

As if realizing someone was there, the horse looked her way. A couple of side steps later, it poked its head over the door beside her and let out a low breathy sound. If Brady were here, he'd be able to tell her what it meant.

She tentatively reached a hand toward its nose. "M-may I pet you?"

Whether on purpose or coincidence, the horse nodded.

Smiling, Kirsten stroked its soft muzzle, realizing how jealous her boys would be if they saw her right now. They'd be back on that stool, asking to do the same.

The thought made her smile.

Brady was right—she was overprotective. Losing her father to cancer had dented her faith. Losing Scott had her questioning how God could do that to her and her mother. And when Brady left, Kirsten was just plain angry with both him and God. Then she found out she was pregnant, and her heart softened—toward God, anyway. But when it came to trusting Him, her faith was still on shaky ground.

Lord, thank you for protecting Trevor. I'm still afraid, though. Please, keep my boys safe. And help me to trust You more.

* * *

Brady exited his truck Friday afternoon, allowing Daisy to bound out behind him before he retrieved the large bag containing three riding helmets from the passenger seat. While the yellow Lab romped around the yard, Brady started toward the barn, determined to prove to Kirsten he cared about their sons every bit as much as she did. He may have arrived late to the game, but from that first moment he'd laid eyes on them, something innate had sprang to life inside Brady. Something fierce and unwavering. Unfamiliar yet instinctive. Love in its purest form. He would never put the boys in a dangerous situation.

Baby steps, he reminded himself as he continued through the barn door. Kirsten had been flying solo for so long she was afraid to let someone else take the controls. Yet, she had agreed to let him start teaching the boys horsemanship, and he wouldn't take that for granted.

He hung the bag from a hook outside the tack room before continuing toward the opposite end of the barn, eyeing the empty stalls along the way. Since he had today off, and Kirsten had only a half day of training, they'd agreed this afternoon would be the perfect time to begin that instruction. And maybe, if he got things right, provide a nice diversion for Kirsten.

Though the urgent care center had yet to open, she seemed busier than a squirrel in a nut factory, scurrying around, trying to make sure everything was just right, both at home and the urgent care. Leaving him to wonder how she was going to manage everything when the urgent care center finally opened its doors.

"I just want everything to go smoothly," she'd told him the other night as she juggled the boys' bedtime with kitchen cleanup and laundry. "My future depends on it."

The woman was determined to do it all. And while Brady understood her desire to succeed, he didn't like seeing her stressed. He wished there were some way he could intercept one or two of those balls she struggled to keep in the air.

Not that he had a lot of time on his hands. Along with his regular shifts this week, he'd spent Tuesday in court testifying in a case, and then Wednesday evening, he'd spoken at the meeting of a local service organization. Only the first of several speaking engagements for his campaign, including a town hall the local Christian women's organization was hosting in March. And he still had a fundraising event to plan.

While Brady didn't mind the various meetings, between the preparation and the event itself, they cut into his time with the twins. Feeding the horses wasn't the same without his little helpers.

Still, he'd managed to drop by Kirsten's and see them every evening, if for nothing more than a short time before they went to bed. Which made today's time together even more special. And he could hardly wait.

At the end of the aisle, he slid open the doors, welcoming the sun's warmth on his face as he breathed in the crisp air. His goal today was to ease Kirsten's angst over the boys being around the horses. And the best way he knew to do that was to get her back in the saddle. To remind her of how she'd once enjoyed riding. Then, if she felt comfortable, perhaps they'd take the boys for a ride in the pasture. Though Brady wasn't holding his breath. After the way Kirsten had reacted Sunday, he knew he'd best proceed with caution. And not only with the horses.

Holding her in his arms had reminded him how easy and natural things had once been between them. It didn't matter if they were riding horses at his dad's place, enjoying the nightlife in College Station or simply curled up on the couch watching a movie, life was just better when they were together. And if he were honest with himself, he'd missed that. More than he realized.

Shaking off the thought, he peered out over the pasture to find Digger heading his way.

"Hey, fella." Dormant grass crackled beneath his boots as he moved to greet the horse, reaching out to rub Digger's neck. "You've been waiting for me, haven't you?" The two of them always went for a ride on Brady's days off. There was nothing quite like being atop a horse to help solve the problems of the world. Sadly, there wasn't as much time to do that in the winter. He'd sure be glad when the days grew longer.

Brady's phone rang and he pulled it from his belt, a jolt of excitement racing through him when he saw Kirsten's name on the screen. "Hello?"

"Just letting you know I have the boys and we are on our way. I just need to stop by the house and change. Anything the boys need to bring?"

"Boots, if they have them. Or something you don't mind getting dirty."

After a slight pause, she said, "Will rubber boots be okay?"

"Yes." Though he made a mental note to find out what sizes they wore so he could pick them up some proper boots.

"We'll see you shortly, then."

His anticipation grew as he returned the phone to its clip. Horses had always been a part of his life, save for his time in the military. So having the opportunity to share that passion with his sons made him happier than a pig in the mud.

Returning his attention to Digger, he scratched the paint's chin. "We're going to need Lucy, too." The docile mare would be a good fit for Kirsten. Because even if she didn't consent to a ride with the boys, he still planned to get *her* back in the saddle.

By the time Kirsten and the twins arrived, both Digger and Lucy were saddled and waiting in the

round pen near the barn. Arms perched on the top
rail, Brady watched as Jeremy and Trevor raced
toward him, their enthusiasm bubbling over into
happy squeals. Something Brady could definitely
appreciate. The horses, not so much.

He maneuvered his frame through the pipe rails
to greet them. "Hey, fellas."

Wearing a gray Henley beneath his red jacket,
Trevor looked up at him. "Are you going to teach
us to ride horses?"

Brady glanced at Kirsten as she brought up the
rear, wondering what she had told them. "I don't
know about that, but I am going to teach you a
few things about horses."

"Like what?" Trevor appeared surprisingly serious.

Kneeling to their level, Brady said, "For starters, what have I told you about running around the
horses? That can scare them. And a scared horse
is unpredictable."

"What's unpre—detable?"

Brady couldn't help but grin at Jeremy's pro-
nunciation. "It means we don't know how they
will react." He looked up as Kirsten joined them,
his breath catching. Bootcut jeans and a flannel
shirt had never looked so good. Even when they
were paired with pink cowboy boots that were
more about style than function.

He touched the brim of his Stetson. "You
dressed the part. I like it."

She eyed her boots before striking a pose. "Even if I'm a rhinestone cowgirl?"

"You wear it well." Distractingly so.

He rubbed his hands together. "All right, before we get started, I have something for each of you." He motioned for them to follow them to the barn.

"What is it?" Trevor asked.

"You'll find out in a second." Inside the barn, he retrieved the bag he'd left there earlier. Reaching inside, he pulled out the blue helmet first and handed it to Jeremy. "These are riding helmets." He handed the red one to Trevor. "They protect your noggin." Finally, he passed a black one to Kirsten, adding, "Thought it might make you feel a little more comfortable." Glancing at her boots, he added, "But now I'm thinking I should've gotten you a pink one."

The smile she gave him went straight to his heart. "Thank you for understanding."

"How come you don't have a helmet?" asked Trevor.

"Oh. Uh…" Brady hadn't anticipated that.

He was still trying to come up with a response when Kirsten said, "Because he's a cowboy. He's been working with horses his whole life."

"That's right. My parents taught me how to ride and care for horses when I was younger than you. And now I'm going to teach you." Even though they had no idea he was their father. Still, it meant a lot that Kirsten had agreed to let him share his passion with the boys.

Once the twins' helmets were on and properly adjusted, he moved to check on Kirsten's. When her big hazel eyes met his, he noticed the fear and uncertainty that had been there Sunday were absent.

Checking the strap, he said, "You okay?"

The corners of her mouth lifted ever so slightly. "Of course. We've got a great teacher."

Her words bolstered him as they moved into the pen to go over some basics with the boys. Before long—and much to his surprise—Kirsten was atop Lucy with Jeremy while Brady and Trevor had settled into Digger's saddle, and they were making their way around the pen. He had Kirsten practice a few times, in hopes of building her confidence.

After an hour of instruction, Kirsten looked his way. "It's such a beautiful day. Why don't we ride in the pasture so you can show us your property?"

"Yeah!" The boys pumped their fists. But then, Brady wouldn't have expected anything less. Having Kirsten feel confident enough to ask, though, was a gift.

"We can do that." He may have sounded calm, but inside he was jumping up and down. This was what he'd wanted. To bring his sons into his world, to experience life *with* him instead of having them watch from the bleachers. He wanted to be a real father to them. And, maybe, even rebuild his relationship with their mother. Because while he may not be worthy, she still held his heart. Was it possible they could be a real family someday?

He opened the pen, aware that he was putting the cart before the horse. Yet, the hope that had sprang to life inside him refused to be squelched. Especially as they made their way into the pasture, the sun shining down on them.

Daisy followed, scampering on ahead.

"It's so peaceful out here." Smiling, Kirsten seemed to take it all in. "I love these majestic oak trees."

"That was part of the appeal. Took me a while to find this place."

"But you were patient. You had a dream, and you didn't settle until you found it."

And as they eased the horses atop a gentle bluff that allowed him to survey his little kingdom, his desire to share his dream with his sons nearly overwhelmed him.

Kirsten sighed. "This looks just the way I envisioned when you used to describe the kind of place you were looking for."

Back when they were dating, Kirsten would listen while he droned on about finding that perfect piece of property to call his own. Then he'd listen when she expressed her desires to have her own clinic someday. Though neither of them imagined it would be in Hope Crossing.

"I guess we both achieved our dreams." At least those they'd discussed. She'd never known about the times he'd allowed his mind to wander, contemplating a life with her. Wondering what it would be like to wake up to her smiling face every day. To go off to work, knowing she'd be there when he came home. To do life together, come what may. And he'd almost fooled himself into believing it might be possible. Until she started talking about children.

That had been the reality check he'd needed.

Now, here they were with the two boys they'd created. And he wanted nothing more than to be a real father to them.

He glanced at Kirsten sitting atop Lucy as though she belonged there. Belonged here. With him.

The buzz of his phone had him shaking off the notion. He'd had his chance with Kirsten. And he'd blown it.

Retrieving the device from his belt, he noted the Houston number. "Hello."

"May I speak with Brady James, please?" the female voice asked.

"This is Brady."

"Hi. My name is Monica, I'm with the health center in Houston. I'm calling to remind you about your appointment Wednesday." She continued, talking about arrival times and what to expect, but Brady barely heard a word. Because just when he felt as though he was truly living, his life, his dreams were again overshadowed by the threat of Huntington's.

He'd said he would never put the boys in danger. But if he tested positive, there was nothing he could do to prevent it.

Chapter Seven

Kirsten watched Brady's smile evaporate. He held the phone to his ear, his shoulders sagging as though some invisible weight pressed down on him. Whoever was on the other end of that call was giving him some unwelcome news. Was it something to do with his work? Or his father?

Ending the call, he returned the phone to its clip.

"Everything okay?" She urged Lucy forward so she could see his face, but the brim of his hat cast a shadow over his features, making it difficult to get a good read.

He cleared his throat, squaring his shoulders once again. "Yeah. We should, uh, probably think about heading back to the barn, though."

"Aww." Trevor frowned. "I want to ride more."

"Me, too," Jeremy whined.

She gave her son's arm a comforting squeeze before addressing the man beside her. "Did something happen? Do you need to leave?"

"No. It's just…" He grimaced, closing his eyes

momentarily. Then, with an almost imperceptible shake of his head, he said, "Come on." He
urged his horse down the gentle slope, continuing deeper into the property instead of toward the
house, much to the boys' delight. Not to mention
her own. She'd forgotten how good being atop a
horse felt. Though she was apt to be sore later.

The twins giggled when Daisy chased a squirrel up a tree, then stood on her hind legs, paws
against the trunk, staring into the branches and
barking as if demanding the squirrel come back
and play with her.

Brady remained quiet, though, his smile not
quite reaching his eyes. Whatever that phone call
was about had completely changed his demeanor.
And she wanted to know why.

Thankfully, the boys didn't seem to notice. Too
many distractions, she supposed. They called
out to Butterscotch, Chief and Nutmeg as they
passed, attempting to engage them in conversation, though their efforts were lost on the horses.

A short time later, Brady stopped them, silently
pointing out a majestic buck. They watched in awe
as the beautiful creature darted across their path
and leaped effortlessly over the fence.

Yet through it all, Brady seemed lost in his
thoughts. Not at all like the man who'd been anticipating this opportunity the way a kid counts
down the days to their birthday.

Memories of that morning at her apartment five

years ago tumbled through her mind. How he'd changed overnight.

She stiffened her spine. If he turned his back on the boys the way he had her…

The sun had begun its trek toward the horizon when Brady said, "We'd best head on back. It'll be dark soon."

Once again, the boys voiced their displeasure, but she ignored it this time. She needed to talk to Brady and find out what was troubling him. Though it wouldn't be easy with the boys around. Especially after what happened Sunday.

Approaching the barn, she noticed Hank filling the water trough outside the barn.

He waved when he spotted them. "I wondered where everyone was." He came alongside Lucy, smiling as his gaze darted between Jeremy and Trevor. "How was the ride, fellas?"

"We sawed a *big* deer." Jeremy held his arms wide.

"Is that so?" Hank reached for the boy to help him down.

"And Daisy chased a squirrel up a tree." Trevor tittered as Hank moved alongside Digger.

"Sounds like y'all had a good time." Reaching for Trevor, the man eyed his son, his gaze narrowing slightly. Did he suspect something was bothering Brady?

While Brady and Kirsten dismounted, the boys chattered nonstop while Hank hung on their every word. Though they quickly shifted gears from their ride to all the toys Brady had bought for them, giving Kirsten an idea.

"Hank, would you mind entertaining the boys while Brady and I untack the horses?"

"You don't have to—" Brady started, only to be interrupted by his father.

"I'd be happy to." Hank motioned to the boys. "Come on, fellas."

They'd just started toward the house when Brady looked her way. "You can go with them. I'll take care of the horses."

She shook her head. "Not a chance. We need to talk." Turning, she led Lucy into the barn.

Amid the earthy scents of horse, leather and hay, Kirsten removed her helmet and hung it on a hook outside of Lucy's stall, aware of Brady's gaze boring into her.

"What do you want to talk about?"

She sucked in a breath, willing herself to remain calm, yet failing miserably. "You can ditch the clueless act, Brady." She faced him. "Everything was going great out there until you got that phone call. You've been sullen ever since." Still holding the reins, she glared up at him. "Reminds me of the day we broke up. Everything was fine, and then it was as though a switch had flipped and you were a different person."

His nostrils flared. His ocean eyes darting around the barn.

She wasn't about to let his annoyance stop her this time. "I loved you, and you didn't even have the decency to tell me the truth. You made me question everything I believed about you. About us! As though our whole relationship had been a lie."

"The only person I was lying to, Kirsten, was myself. First believing I could have a future with you, and then thinking I would get over you." He shook his head, still refusing to meet her gaze. "What we had was the kind of stuff dreams are made of. But when I woke up that morning, I was reminded of the nightmare my life might turn into. And I couldn't do that to you."

Dropping the reins, she took a step closer. Lifted her chin, daring him to look at her. When he finally did, she said, "I guess you think that makes you some kind of hero, huh? Sparing me from heartache."

He started to answer, but she cut him off. "Well, guess again." Realizing she'd revealed just how much he'd hurt her, she quickly forged on. "You insisted you wanted to be a part of the boys' lives. Tell me, are you going to shut them out, the way you did me? Because I will not allow you to hurt them." The pain she'd endured was bad enough. Watching her sons go through that would be even worse. "So you tell me, Brady, which way is it going to be? Because there's no middle ground here. You're either all in or all out when it comes to Jeremy and Trevor."

He was quiet for a long while, his gaze everywhere but on her, his Adam's apple bobbing at a frenzied pace. Finally, he heaved a sigh and peered down at her. "That phone call was from the health center in Houston, reminding me of my appointment next week."

"And that's a problem?"

"More like a reminder." Lifting his hat briefly, he raked his fingers through his hair. "These past two weeks, spending time with the twins, has made me feel—different. Like I finally had a purpose. One that mattered. More than being a deputy, or even sheriff. Being with them has made me happier than I've been in years." He lowered his head. "That phone call reminded me all of that could be snatched away if I have Huntington's."

Trying hard to ignore the fact that the twins had given him a purpose and happiness while she hadn't, she stared up at him, shaking her head. "So you'd rather give up that happiness because you *might*—" she made air quotes with her fingers "—have Huntington's, rather than experiencing all life has to offer you for as long as possible? I'm sorry, Brady, but that's some messed up logic. That's like saying you're not going to drive a car because you might have an accident. Was that how your mother lived?"

He turned away, shaking his head as he began

loosening the straps on Digger's saddle. "According to Dad, she said time was too precious to waste doing something she wasn't passionate about."

Kirsten watched him tend the horse. "Those are some wise words for all of us."

His hands stilled. "I suppose. But watching my mom deteriorate, not understanding why she would shut herself in her bedroom because depression was getting the best of her, or the uncontrolled movements or difficulty speaking." He shook his head. "That's what I remember."

Her heart ached for the confused boy he must've been. No doubt about it, Huntington's was a cruel disease. "Perhaps it's time you start remembering some of the good things about your mother."

He lifted his head to look at her now. "That first night I came to your place for supper, Jeremy asked if I had any dinosaurs, and I was reminded of this book I used to beg my mom to read to me over and over." He cleared his throat. "For a moment, I remembered the warmth of her embrace and her rose-scented perfume."

Kirsten had to blink away the tears that sprang to her eyes. "What a precious memory. That's what you need to dwell on, Brady, not the negative stuff." Despite her head telling her to keep her distance, she inched closer to him. "While it seems much longer, it was only last week you told me you couldn't turn your back on your children. So what's it going to be? Are you going to allow a what-if to keep you from living life to its fullest, or are you going to embrace the blessings God has given you?"

"And if the what-if turns into a for-sure?"

While she didn't want to think about that, "Then you'll continue to make memories with those who love you."

"Mama! Mama!"

Clearing her throat, she turned at the twins' happy voices echoing from the other end of the barn.

"Mr. Hank said we could have pizza for dinner." Trevor's smile was wide.

"If it's okay with you," Jeremy clarified. "Can we?"

Hank strolled up behind them. "Sorry. I probably shouldn't have said anything before checking with you, Kirsten. But if you haven't got anything planned, I'd be happy to go pick up some carry-out."

She couldn't help but recognize what an amazing grandfather the boys had in Hank. He would spoil them for sure. "I think that sounds like a wonderful idea." She glanced at the man beside her. "What do you say, Brady?"

"Sounds good to me. I'll go ahead and order on my phone, so it'll be ready when you get there, Dad."

She watched as Brady made note of everyone's

preferences, glad she'd confronted him. But she also recognized she was going to have to watch herself. It would be far too easy to fall for Brady again.

No, that wasn't correct. Because that would mean she'd gotten over him. And while she'd like to kid herself into believing that was true, she knew that wasn't the case. There was a part of her heart that still belonged to Brady. She just had to make sure he never found it.

Perhaps Kirsten and his father were right. That Brady should stop dwelling on the negative memories of his mother and make an effort to recall the positive ones.

Scratch that. They *were* right. His mother would be sad if she knew Brady had allowed a few difficult years to overshadow the good times they'd once shared. Now he wanted to start building memories with his sons. Something that seemed easier after last night.

While Dad had gone to pick up the pizzas, Brady, Kirsten and the twins untacked, groomed and fed the horses before gathering wood for the firepit in Brady's backyard. Then they'd enjoyed their supper under the stars as a family, amid firelight, easy conversation and the antics of two little boys. He couldn't recall a more perfect evening.

Thanks to an overnight cold front, though, he couldn't say the same about today.

In the cool, damp air outside his friend and former classmate Jake Walker's hay barn early the next morning, Brady secured straps around both square and round bales of hay loaded on the flatbed trailer behind his truck while Daisy supervised.

"Will you be at church tomorrow?" Hands tucked in the pockets of his camo softshell, Jake watched him.

"Not this week." Mission accomplished, Brady hopped down to join his friend under the barn's overhang. "I'm on duty tomorrow." Since his first doctor appointment was in Houston Wednesday, he'd traded shifts with another deputy.

Nodding, Jake toed at the dirt with his worn work boots. "I, uh, couldn't help noticing you had a friend with you last Sunday. A mighty pretty one, too." The glint in Jake's eyes, along with a smirk, told Brady his buddy was fishing. "We don't usually see you around the nursery."

Brady wasn't about to give Jake the satisfaction of even the slightest nibble. Crossing his arms over his chest, he said, "That was my friend Kirsten. She was picking up her twin boys." *His* twin boys. He wasn't free to say that, though. Not when Jeremy and Trevor still had no idea. Though after last night, the thought seemed to cross his mind more and more.

Jake eyed him in earnest now. "Alli says she's a doctor or something at that new urgent care center we've all been looking forward to. I hear she came from College Station." Jake's wife, Alli, was the director of Hope Crossing's one and only child care center, so it made sense she'd know a few more details about Kirsten.

Not everything, though. "Yes, she's a nurse practitioner."

Another annoying grin had Jake's brow lifting. "Which begs the question, how do *you* know her?"

Brady snorted, dropping his arms. "Her brother and I were army buddies." Not a lie. Just not the whole truth.

"Oh." Jake frowned. Typical newlywed. Caught up in wedded bliss, thinking his friends should be doing the same.

"Sorry to disappoint you, man." Though he'd be lying if he said he wasn't a tad envious of his friend who'd married last summer and now had a baby on the way. A nice addition to the two kiddos from Jake's first marriage.

The sound of sporadic raindrops hitting the barn's metal roof had Brady surveying the gloomy sky once again. "I'd best get out of here before things let loose." He shook his friend's hand. "Thanks, man." Starting toward his truck, he hollered, "Come on, Daisy girl."

He opened the door and she bounded into the cab ahead of him. Once he started the engine, he promptly cranked up the heat.

Sprinkles dotted the windshield as he pulled

away from the Walker ranch. Hopefully it wouldn't rain in earnest until after the hay was unloaded. Though with the darkening clouds, he'd have to work quickly.

His phone rang and *Dad* appeared on the Bluetooth screen on his dash. He touched the appropriate icon. "Hey, Dad."

"You get that hay?"

"On my way home now."

"Need some help unloading?"

"Absolutely."

"I'm on my way."

By the time Brady came to a stop alongside the galvanized metal structure that had been on his property since the house was built in the 1920s and now served as his hay barn, his father's truck was right behind him.

They immediately set to work offloading the square bales manually. A task that had them both shedding their jackets. Thankfully, the rain was only a fine mist. Once they were done, Brady stacked them inside the barn, while Dad fired up the tractor to offload the round bales that were for the pasture.

Once the task was completed, it didn't take long for the cold to start seeping into their bones. Temps were supposed to tumble into the twenties overnight, so Brady would need to prepare the horses accordingly. Put out extra hay, blanket them…

"A steaming hot cup of coffee would really hit

the spot." Standing just inside the barn, watching mist fall from the sky, Dad burrowed his hands in the pockets of his brown Carhartt jacket.

"Yeah, it would. And I just happen to have some kolaches, too. Care to join me?"

"Lead the way."

A short time later, they'd settled around Brady's kitchen table, steam rising from their mugs.

"I sure enjoyed last night." Dad smiled. "Looked like you were having a good time, too."

Brady picked at his fruit-filled pastry, grinning at the memory. "Yeah, it was nice." Sitting under the stars with Jeremy and Trevor, pointing out the different constellations had felt so right. Like he was a real dad.

"Son, there's something I need to tell you. Something I think you need to know."

He eyed his father, who'd grown suddenly serious. "What's that?"

Both hands wrapped around his mug, Dad rested his elbows on the table. "Your mama and I. We never planned to have any children. We took all the precautions—or thought we had—yet here you sit."

Brady straightened, staring at the man. "How come I never knew this?"

His father shrugged. "Didn't seem pertinent."

"No, I suppose not." Still… "How'd Mama react when she found out she was pregnant?" Had she had the same fears as Brady?

Dad set his drink on the table and leaned back in his chair. "Once she got over the shock, she said, 'This baby wasn't by our design, Hank, but by God's. So I can't help thinking He's got something special in store for him or her.'" The man's gaze was as riveted to Brady's as Brady's was to his. "You were an unexpected gift, son. And you brought your mama so much joy, even on her worst days. The times when the depression was trying to get the best of her and you'd go in and read to her, or simply sit and hold her hand and tell her you loved her. You brightened those dark moments and made them bearable for her."

The comment unearthed a memory. Something Brady hadn't thought about in a very long time. He was around twelve and had to miss a friend's birthday party because his mom was in a bad way and Dad didn't want to leave her. At his father's urging, a moping Brady had gone into her room and sat with her. Obviously sensing his disappointment, tears filled her eyes. She was as upset as he was that he'd missed the party on account of her. Nonetheless, he'd told her it was okay and passed her a tissue.

After collecting herself, and despite her slurred, often slow speech, she began asking him questions. What he wanted to do when he grew up. Why? All sorts of inquiries about his hopes and dreams. They'd talked for hours. He'd made his mama smile. And he had smiled, too.

Strange, he'd never realized it before, but now he understood why she'd done it. She'd wanted him to dream. To reach for the stars, even though she knew she might not be here to see him achieve those dreams. But that day, she was able to imagine him doing those things he'd told her he'd do.

How many of them had he actually done, though? When had he stopped dreaming and started just going through the motions of life?

Sadly, he knew the answer. It was that day he walked out of Kirsten's apartment, never imagining what he'd be missing out on.

Did he dare dream again?

The thought beckoned him like a cold crystal stream on a hot summer day.

"Earth to Brady."

He lifted his gaze to find his father staring at him.

"Where'd you go?"

"Just thinking about Mama."

His father smiled. "You know, son, even if you were to have Huntington's, you are still fearfully and wonderfully made. God's word says so. Now the choice is up to you. Are you going to take God at His word and live the life He has planned for you or not?"

The temptation to say yes took root and began to grow. He wanted to be a real father to Jeremy and Trevor. To build memories with them.

If anything happens to me, Bro, promise you'll take care of Kirsten.

Of course, Brady had told Scott, never imagining it would actually happen. After all, it was only a training exercise.

Even now, he remembered the intensity in Scott's eyes. Had he sensed something was going to happen?

Now Scott was gone, but Brady was still here.

He had always thought of himself as honorable. Even back in high school when he'd taken the fall for Gloriana. Breaking into the ag barn may not have been his idea, but he hadn't tried to stop her, either. Instead, he'd gone along with her plan. Then taken the blame and paid the consequences.

So what about the promise he'd made to Scott?

Brady could only shake his head. He'd failed his friend—and, in turn, Kirsten and his sons.

Some sense of honor.

Brady had allowed Huntington's to control him without even knowing if he had it. Perhaps it was time to step out from under the canopy of fear that had hovered over him since that day he walked out on Kirsten and wholeheartedly embrace the unexpected blessings God had brought him. Maybe even dream again.

His greatest obstacle was going to be convincing Kirsten he meant it this time.

Chapter Eight

Kirsten pulled up to the single-story brick building that housed the Hope Crossing fire station, town hall and library Saturday morning, thankful Alli Walker, the director at the early learning center, had mentioned the Children's Story Hour to her earlier in the week. On this cold dreary morning, it was just the motivation she'd needed to get herself and the boys out of the house. Otherwise, Jeremy and Trevor would still be in their pajamas, staring at the television while she was curled up on the sofa with another cup of coffee, mentally dissecting her conversation with Brady yesterday.

Their time together had started off so well. Brady had gone out of his way to help her overcome her fears. The fact that he'd bought her and the boys helmets had threatened to turn her into a puddle. He'd put her at ease, rekindled her love of riding and made her want to share that with the twins as much as he did.

Then he received that phone call. Thankfully,

the boys had been oblivious to the shift in his demeanor. Yet, while Brady had never answered her question after Hank interrupted them in the barn, his actions seemed to indicate he wasn't ready to give up on fatherhood, after all. On the contrary, between the pizza, the campfire and wonderful conversation, the rest of the evening was one to remember. Save for the litany of what-ifs the splendid night stirred inside her.

Now she pushed her SUV door open and stepped into the cold drizzle, moving quickly to the back door to let the boys out.

"Ms. Alli reads to us at school." Jeremy peered up at her, blinking against the misty air while they waited for Trevor to exit. "She's a good reader."

"Do they have any dinosaur books here?" Trevor leaped from the back seat.

"I'm sure they do." Kirsten closed the door behind him. "They might not read one today, but we can always check out some to bring home."

Her boys shared excited grins, then gave a collective, "Yay!"

Holding each of their hands, she approached the entrance. "I want you both to be on your best behavior. Inside voices, please. And when Ms. Alli is reading, you need to sit on your bottoms and listen, okay?"

"Okay," they echoed.

She pulled the glass door open, and they stepped

inside to find Alli talking with an auburn-haired woman.

Looking up, Alli smiled. "You came!" She approached them, her blue eyes falling to the boys. "I'm so happy to see you. And Maddy will be, too." She pointed to the area left of the door with kid-height bookshelves and a colorful rug where a girl close to the boys' age with blond ponytails sat reading a book while a younger white-blond boy looked on beside her.

Alli glanced over her shoulder to the woman she'd been talking to. "Jillian, I have someone I'd like you to meet."

As the woman started their way, Kirsten noticed the chocolate-brown poodle with a service vest at her side.

"Jillian, this is Kirsten Reynolds and her sons, Jeremy and Trevor." Alli set a hand atop her baby bump. "Kirsten is the nurse practitioner at the new urgent care."

Jillian's blue eyes widened. "I'm so glad to meet you." She held out her hand and Kirsten briefly took hold. "I have a six-week-old, so we may be seeing each other a lot in the future."

"Well, we offer well-baby checkups, in addition to diagnosing general illnesses."

"Jillian is our library director," Alli added.

"In that case, I expect we'll be seeing each other quite a bit," said Kirsten.

"Why is your dog wearing that?" Ever inquisitive, Jeremy pointed to the poodle's vest.

Jillian turned her attention to the boys. "Aggie is my service dog. Her vest lets people know she's working."

"It also means you're not allowed to pet or play with her while she's wearing her vest," Kirsten added.

"Oh." The boys' eyes were wide now. And Kirsten knew she'd likely be fielding questions all the way home.

A petite blonde entered then, accompanied by a dark-haired boy Kirsten guessed to be around the twins' age.

"Hello, Tori." Jillian's gaze moved to the boy. "Are you ready for Story Hour, young man?"

Trevor tugged Kirsten's right hand. "That's Aiden."

"He's in our class," Jeremy added from her left.

The blonde smiled their way. Leaning toward the boy who was with her, she said, "Are these the twins you've been telling me about?"

He nodded.

"Are you here for Story Hour, too?" Trevor asked his friend.

Aiden smiled. "Uh-huh."

"We've never been here before." Jeremy's voice was quiet.

Standing a little taller, Aiden smiled. "It's fun.

C'mon." Motioning for the twins to follow, he started toward Alli's children.

Her boys looked up at her. "Can we?"

"Sure."

As the boys took off, Jillian said, "Tori, have you and Kirsten met?"

"We have not." Tori smiled Kirsten's way. "But I've heard a lot about your boys. I think Aiden is a little envious that he doesn't have a twin."

"Trust me, it's not for the faint of heart," said Kirsten.

"I imagine. I can barely handle one." Tori lifted a shoulder. "Just as well since I'm a single mom."

"Me, too." Kirsten was thrilled to connect with someone who understood the same challenges she faced.

"Really?" Tori's blue eyes grew even wider. "Oh, honey, you've got your work cut out for you, don't you?"

"I suppose. But given that I don't know anything else..." Kirsten shrugged.

"We definitely need to get to know each other." Tori looped an arm through Kirsten's. "Let's find a place to sit."

They found a table far enough away that they were able to carry on a conversation, yet close enough to keep an eye on the boys.

"It must've been tough leaving College Station, knowing you were losing your support system. I mean, at least I have my mother-in-law and brother-in-law."

Kirsten couldn't help thinking about Brady and Hank. Not only how good they were with the boys, but how eager they were to help. Of course, Brady hadn't given her an answer yesterday. Though they say actions speak louder than words. If that were the case, he'd said an awful lot around that campfire. The way he engaged with the boys, sometimes acting like a kid himself.

"So far it hasn't been too bad. My late brother's best friend lives here, and he's been a big help."

"That's good. What's his name?"

Kirsten hoped she wasn't opening a can of worms. "Brady James."

Tori stared at her for a long moment. "Really? Brady and I went to school together. He was a year behind me, but in Hope Crossing, everyone knows everyone." Across from her, Tori rested her cardigan-covered arms atop the table and leaned closer. "You wouldn't know it now, but he was painfully shy back then. Kind of a lost-puppy-dog sort."

"You're kidding." Brady's confidence was one of the things Kirsten had always admired about him.

Tori nodded. "He kind of stuck to himself. Looking back, I think it was because of his mother. She had some brain disease—I forget the name—that affected her ability to function normally." Lifting a shoulder, she added, "She died pretty young."

"That's too bad." Kirsten could only imagine how confused and alone Brady must have felt. Kids don't understand that sort of stuff. Nor do they like to feel different. Which explained a lot about his fears over Huntington's. Not only for himself, but for the twins.

"But between military school and the military itself," Tori continued, "Brady found his confidence. Did he tell you he's running for sheriff?"

"Yes, he did."

Laughter had them both turning toward the kids.

Kirsten's gaze found Jeremy and Trevor sitting cross-legged on the rug with eight other children, their eyes fixed on Alli as she read *The Cat in the Hat* in a very animated manner.

How would the twins react if they knew Brady was their father, built a relationship with him and then he began to deteriorate the way his mother had? It was a jarring thought, for sure. But then, what if she were in Brady's shoes? Would she want to close herself off from those she loved?

Thoughts of her father came to mind. No matter how sick he'd been or how out of it he was, he always smiled when he heard her, her mother's or Scott's voices. Even unconscious, he was aware of their presence and that he was surrounded by love.

Everyone deserved to know they were loved. That there were people who would rally around them, no matter what. Including Brady.

Her phone vibrated in her pocket. Retrieving it, she saw a text from the man himself.

Would you like some company?

We're at the library for Story Hour. Her thumbs hovered over the screen as she contemplated whether or not to invite Brady to join them.

Deciding against it, she hit Send.

Smiling at Tori, she said, "So tell me about you."

In short order, she learned that Tori was an elementary school teacher and a widowed military wife. Like Jeremy and Trevor, Aiden had never known his father. Contrary to Aiden's circumstances, though, the twins still had the opportunity to build a relationship with theirs.

Kirsten swallowed around the unexpected lump in her throat. What would Tori think of her if she knew Kirsten had deliberately not told Brady about the twins?

Suddenly, her reasoning seemed rather selfish.

As the kids gathered around tables to color, Tori looked somewhere beyond Kirsten, her smile growing. "Well, look who's here."

Kirsten turned to find Brady coming toward them, looking like the confident soldier she'd once fallen head over heels for. Especially when he shifted his gaze to the boys.

"Hey, Tori," he said as he approached.

"Hey, yourself. How's the campaign going?"

His smile grew wider. "Just trying to get the word out."

"If you have any signs, I'd be happy to put one in my yard."

"Great. I do have some. I just haven't distributed them yet. I'll put you at the top of my list."

"Mr. Brady?"

Both he and Kirsten turned at Jeremy's voice.

"Hey, buddy." Brady squatted beside him, his gaze falling to the paper in Jeremy's hands. "Whatcha got there?"

"A horsey. It's s'posed to be Lucy, 'cept I used the wrong color."

Brady ruffled the boy's dark hair that was so like his own. "I don't know. I think it looks pretty good."

"But I didn't do her spots."

"Aw, that's easy to fix." Brady pushed to his feet and held out his hand. "Come on, I'll show you."

Kirsten watched them walk away, smiling. She appreciated the way Brady always encouraged the boys.

"He's such a good guy," she heard Tori say.

"He is." Or at least he tried to be. Until his fears had him taking a step back. Not so unlike herself. Yet while she was aware of Brady's motivations, the thought of him running hot and cold with the boys left her cautious.

Kirsten faced Tori again as the other woman's blue eyes shifted from Brady to her. Tori folded her arms atop the table and leaned closer.

"You said Brady was your late-brother's friend?"

Kirsten shifted in her own seat, gripping its edges as she nodded. "Mmm-hmm." The half-truth made her stomach churn. She shouldn't have told Brady where she was.

Clasping her hands together, Tori leaned closer. "Kirsten, I know we just met, and you owe me no explanations." She glanced around, as if making sure they were alone, a move that had Kirsten fidgeting. Then, in a whispered voice, Tori said, "Is Brady the twins' father?"

It wasn't like Brady to be nervous. But then, his entire life was about to change in a big way. At least, he hoped so.

With Story Hour over, he helped the twins collect the pictures they'd colored, then started toward Kirsten who was still sitting with Tori. In front of him, Jeremy and Trevor flanked Aiden as they shuffled toward the two women, all the while discussing their favorite superheroes.

Another glance to where Kirsten and Tori sat revealed the two women huddled across the table, seemingly deep in conversation. So deeply, they appeared surprised when they saw the boys.

"Are you guys finished already?" Tori straightened.

"Yes," said Aiden.

Hurrying to her feet so fast she almost toppled her chair, Kirsten smiled at the twins. "Did you have fun?" Her voice sounded strange. Higher pitched and way too cheerful. Like someone caught doing something they weren't supposed to.

Not that the boys noticed. Trevor and Aiden nodded, while Jeremy said, "Uh-huh."

Moving closer, Brady touched her elbow. "Everything all right?"

"Of course." She waved him off, nodding repeatedly. "You guys just startled me, that's all."

"Can we go to Mr. Brady's?" Trevor reached for his red fleece jacket.

Kirsten handed Jeremy his blue one. "Oh, I don't—"

"Sure!" Brady managed to catch Kirsten's attention. "There's something I could use your help with." He knelt to aid Trevor with his zipper. "I have an idea for the Boot Scoot'n Barbecue Bash, but I'd like your input. I thought, maybe, we could buzz down to the dance hall for a few minutes so I could go over things with you."

"Oh." Crouched in front of Jeremy, seemingly fixated on his zipper, she said, "I guess that would be all right. It's almost lunchtime, though."

"Not a problem. I brought some snacks to tide the boys over."

Aiden shrugged into his corduroy shirt jacket. "Mama, can Jeremy and Trevor come over and play?"

The twins let go a collective gasp, their gazes colliding momentarily before shifting to Kirsten. "Can we, Mama?"

Tori sent Kirsten a look that seemed to say, *I'm sorry.* "Aiden, I thought you wanted me to see if Uncle Micah was available today."

"But I want to play with Jeremy and Trevor." The boy with dark brown hair and eyes reminiscent of his father and uncle frowned.

"Aiden, it sounds like they already have plans."

Jeremy placed a hand against Kirsten's cheek. "Mama, please. I want to go to Aiden's house."

"Me, too." Trevor pouted.

"Kirsten, I'm fine with them coming over for a couple of hours if you are." Tori looked their way. "I'll feed them lunch and the three of them can wear each other out."

Brady eased Trevor's zipper upward, thinking how nice it would be to discuss things freely with Kirsten without having to worry about the boys overhearing them. But then, Kirsten didn't know Tori all that well. He'd not heard Kirsten mention her before. Still, given the nature of what he wanted to tell Kirsten—more than just the Boot Scoot'n Barbecue Bash, but that he wanted the twins to know he was their father—it might be better if the boys weren't there.

He leaned toward Kirsten and lowered his voice. "Tori's good people. You can trust her."

For a brief moment, Kirsten's eyes searched his and he saw her uncertainty. He stood, holding out a hand to help her up.

She ignored it. And with an almost imperceptible shake of her head, she pushed to her feet.

Brady followed suit as Tori slung her purse over her shoulder.

Biting her lip, Kirsten eyed the other woman. "You're sure?"

"Of course." Tori waved a hand. "They'll have a ball."

Kirsten looked at the boys, then gave a seemingly resigned sigh. "Do you promise to be on your best behavior?"

"Yes." All smiles, the twins bobbed their heads in agreement.

Pulling her phone from the pocket of her jeans, Kirsten caught Tori's eye. "I'll need your phone number and address, along with a promise that you'll call me if they give you any problem whatsoever."

Once the twins' booster seats had been transferred and the boys all buckled into Tori's vehicle with a promise to pick them up at three o'clock, Kirsten and Brady waved goodbye and started for their respective vehicles. Though the drizzle had subsided, the air still had that cold, damp feel. And a breeze out of the north wasn't helping any.

"We may as well ride together," he said. "I can drive."

She looked at him, her brow creasing. "What if there's a problem and I need to get to the boys?"

He couldn't help smiling. While Kirsten was a good mother, she had a tendency to fret a little too much. But then up until recently, her mother and stepdad had been her only support system. Now that she'd moved to Hope Crossing, she was on her own. Not for long, though. At least, not if he had anything to say about it.

"Then I will take you." Touching her elbow, he eased her toward his truck.

Inside the cab, he fired up the engine and cranked up the heat.

Kirsten stared out the window as he pulled out of the parking lot. "So what is it you want to show me?"

"The dance hall where the bash will take place. I figured since you've never seen it, it might be best to give you a visual while I lay out my ideas."

"What sort of ideas?"

He stopped at the blinking red light. "I'll explain when we get there."

Continuing down the two-lane county road, he said, "I sure enjoyed last night. My folks and I used to have supper around a campfire in our backyard when I was little. I'd kind of forgotten, so it was a nice reminder of happier times with my mom." His grip tightened on the steering wheel. "Do you think the boys had fun?"

Her soft chuckle wrapped around his heart. "You mean you couldn't tell? It was all they talked about all the way home and again this morning."

"Oh, yeah? Which part?"

"All of it. Daisy catching their pizza crusts in the air, Hank finding quarters behind their ears, you showing them Orion's Belt."

He felt his smile growing wider with each item she ticked off on her fingers. "I'll have to try and find my old telescope so we can use it the next time."

Her smile faltered then. She turned away to stare out the window.

"Did I say something wrong?"

"No." She hauled in a breath, suddenly engrossed in some black angus huddled around a bale of hay in a winter-weary pasture. "I just don't want you making any promises to the boys that you're not ready to keep."

After what happened during their ride yesterday, he supposed he deserved that. Lord willing, she'd have a little more confidence in him after he told her he was ready to be a real father, come what may.

Eyeing the white clapboard building on the right up ahead, he turned on his blinker, slowing his speed before turning into the gravel drive.

Kirsten straightened. "Is this the dance hall?"

"Sure is." He pulled alongside the historic structure that sat on a pier-and-beam foundation and had a high-pitched metal roof that eased down over the two sides that had been added to the original structure. "One of the oldest in Texas. Though they've recently updated a few things." Turning off the engine, he reached for his door. "Let's go check it out."

The cold air had Kirsten burying her hands in the pockets of her coat while he unlocked the door. Finally, they stepped inside to the lingering aromas of fresh paint and polyurethane.

He flipped the switch for the single-bulb pendant lights dangling throughout the space, his gaze traveling from the exposed rafters to the original wood floors. "Now that the floors have been refinished, the restrooms updated and a commercial kitchen added, the board plans to start renting the place as a venue."

"I can see why." She moved deeper into the building, looking all around the large open space with a stage opposite the entrance. "People pay big bucks for places like this."

"That's what we're banking on." He strode toward her. "The Boot Scoot'n Barbecue Bash is so the community can get a sneak peek."

"Great idea." She faced him now. "Speaking of which, you said you had some ideas for the kids."

"Yes." Motioning for her to follow, he moved

toward the stage. "I'll need to get permission from Gloriana, but here's what I'm thinking." He faced Kirsten now. "What if we created a kids' zone in this corner over here?" He moved to the right of the stage. "We could make it look like a barn or corral. Bring in some hay bales and other ranch-type decorations."

She nodded. "Then what?"

He pulled out his phone. "We already established that the goal is to make the kids feel like they're part of the fun." He scrolled. "So I was thinking we'll have some games, crafts, if you like. And this." He moved beside her and turned his phone so she could see it.

"Stick horses made with wooden yardsticks and posterboard heads?" She cast a wary look his way.

"Yes. The kids get to design—well, color anyway—their horse head. Then, once they're affixed to the sticks, they can do a barrel race." He pointed to the space in front of the stage. "We'd have a couple of barrels out there, then play some music while they galloped around them."

She laughed at his demonstration, the sweet sound reminding him of the fun they used to have together.

Returning to her side, he said, "What do you think?"

"I think it's a great idea. One I'm certain the boys will enjoy."

He heaved a sigh of relief. "Good. I'm glad you

like it. But you're welcome to tweak it if you have any ideas."

"No, not at all." She looked away, her smile fading.

"Hey." He touched her elbow. "You okay?"

It took her a moment, but she finally met his gaze. "Tori knows you're the twins' father."

He couldn't hide his surprise. "You told her?" That would be a step in the right direction.

"No. She figured it out on her own. Just like anyone who sees you with them will." Kirsten exhaled, rubbing her arms as she turned away. "I told her it was a complicated story, that the boys were not aware you're their father and asked her to keep it to herself."

He moved beside her. "Kirsten, my idea for a kids' zone isn't the only reason I wanted to talk to you. I've been thinking about what you said yesterday, and you're right. Jeremy and Trevor are unexpected blessings. And while they weren't a part of my plans, they're a part of God's. I would like to tell the boys that I'm their father. Both of us. Together."

"And what about your campaign?"

He shrugged. "All the more reason to go public. Voters don't like secrets."

Kirsten fell silent.

Breathing in the once-familiar scent of her, he hooked a finger under her chin and urged her to look at him. "Last night was one of the best of my life." He grinned, lifting a shoulder. "In the last five years, anyway."

The blush that crept into her cheeks had him wondering if she could ever forgive him for walking away from her. For hurting her.

"I love them, Kirsten. I want Jeremy and Trevor to know I'm their father."

Her hazel eyes searched his for the longest time. Then she turned away, clutching her arms while she stared at the ceiling. "There's just one problem. They think their father is dead."

He could not have heard her correctly. Moving in front of her, he said, "Say that again."

"A year or so ago, the boys were hounding me, wanting to know why they didn't have a dad like the other kids. I was exasperated and I never thought I'd see you again, so rather than trying to explain something they'd never understand, I told them their daddy died."

All he could do was stare at her. "I can't believe you would do that. Do you have any idea how that makes me feel?"

She glared at him. "As a matter of fact, I do." Fists balled, she continued. "You were adamant about not having children. I was just trying to make the best of a bad situation, because if the boys knew the truth, it would crush their little hearts the way you crushed mine, and I couldn't do that to them."

Brady dragged a hand through his hair, regret

cloaking him once again. He sighed. "You're right. I'm sorry. May I ask you a question, though?"

She looked up at him.

"Why did you come to Hope Crossing then, knowing I'd be here?"

She shrugged. "Having my own clinic was my dream." Her gaze fell away then. "But there was also some small part of me that hoped you might want to be a father to Jeremy and Trevor."

Her words pierced his heart. "Then I guess both of your dreams have come true." He moved in front of her. "Look, do you suppose we could agree to leave our mistakes in the past as we work toward helping the boys adjust to a new norm? One where they have two parents who love them and want what's best for them."

Her lips parted ever so slightly, and for a moment he thought she was going to argue. Then she smiled. "I would like that very much."

Chapter Nine

When Kirsten woke up that morning, she could not have imagined the turn her day would take. Not only had the secret she'd held tightly for almost five years been discovered by someone she'd just met, now she was about to do the one thing she'd only dreamed of, never imagining it would actually transpire.

For the millionth time today, her chest constricted. After agreeing to tell the boys the truth about their father, Brady took her to retrieve her vehicle, then she followed him to his father's where they shared their decision with Hank, who lovingly hugged her and promised to pray over the situation. Then asked if it would be all right for him to stop by later and officially meet his grandsons.

On her way to get the boys, she called her mother to tell her of their decision.

"Oh, honey. That makes me so happy." Mom was crying. "Brady is a good man. I've missed him so much."

Kirsten was still trying to figure that one out

as she stood in her living room a while later, rolling her shoulders, attempting to work out the tension while the boys told Brady everything they'd done at Aiden's.

Hands on his hips, he smiled down at his sons, looking far more relaxed than she felt. How did one tell their children they'd lied to them?

"You two had loads of fun, didn't you?" Brady glanced from one boy to the other.

"Uh-huh," said Trevor. "Want to play dinosaurs?"

Glancing her way, Brady gave a tight smile. "I think your mama has something she wants to talk to you about first."

She drew in a deep breath, the lavender-vanilla candle she had burning failing to calm her as she tugged her cardigan closer. "Yes. Let's, uh, sit down on the sofa, shall we?"

"Are we in trouble?" Beside the coffee table, Jeremy grimaced.

She couldn't help smiling. As wound up as she was, it's no wonder they were concerned. "Not at all." Perching on the edge of the cushion, she patted the one next to her. "I just need to talk to you about something very important."

As the boys crawled beside her, Brady eased onto the opposite end of the sofa, finally having the decency to look nervous. Poor judgment on both their parts had them fearing the worst.

The twins watched her. She and Brady had

agreed she would take the lead. Now she struggled to admit she'd lied to the two people she loved more than life itself.

Lord, I messed up. Please help me get this right.

She smiled at their sweet little faces. "Boys, I made a mistake. I told you something that wasn't true."

Jeremy's jaw dropped. "You lied, Mama?"

Her chest constricting even more, she nodded. Nothing quite as humbling as setting a bad example for your children. "Yes, I did. When I told you your daddy died."

The boys' dark eyebrows scrunched together.

Hands clasped in her lap, she continued. "The truth is he's very much alive, but he never knew about the two of you until recently."

"Why?" Trevor cocked his little head.

Because Brady had hurt her. And she was a coward. Being rejected by him once had been painful enough. A second time would've completely deflated her.

Licking her lips, she glanced at Brady. "I wasn't sure how to tell him or how he would react."

Their confused little faces remained fixed on hers. Did they even comprehend what she was trying to tell them?

Time to rip off the bandage.

"Brady is your daddy."

Both pairs of ocean-blue eyes widened as they twisted toward the man they resembled so much.

Brady nodded. "It's true. And now that I know about the two of you, wild horses couldn't keep me away."

"What's a wild horse?" Jeremy's brow wrinkled.

Brady chuckled. "What I'm trying to say is I love you both very much. And I want us to spend as much time together as possible."

"With the horses?" Trevor's eyes were wide.

"Sometimes," said Brady. "Other times, we'll hang out here."

"Are you going to live with us?" Jeremy asked matter-of-factly.

Meanwhile, Kirsten's cheeks flamed. "No, that wouldn't be appropriate. Your daddy and I aren't married."

"You could get married," said Jeremy. "Then we could always be together."

If only life were that simple.

"Sorry, but no," she said. "However, there's something else you might like."

"What?" Both boys bounced beside her.

"Mr. Hank is Brady's dad. That means he's your grandpa."

Mouths agape, eyes wide with excitement, the boys shared a look.

"Can we call him Grandpa Hank?" Trevor bounced on the cushion.

"You'll have to ask him," said Brady. "But I suspect he'll like that."

Facing his father now, Jeremy said, "Can he come over so we can ask him?"

Laughing, Brady said, "I will text him right now."

"May as well invite him to stay for dinner," said Kirsten. "I've got beef stew in the slow cooker."

Since Hank had remained at Brady's after helping feed the horses, eagerly awaiting the opportunity to claim the title of grandpa, it wasn't long before he joined them.

As usual, the boys had to show him all their toys. Hank took it in stride, though, appearing to revel in every moment.

While Brady and his dad entertained the boys—or, perhaps, vice versa—Kirsten retreated to the kitchen to work on dinner. Rubbing the back of her neck, she turned on the oven, before grabbing a large sheet pan from the cupboard and two cans of dinner rolls from the refrigerator.

To say she was overwhelmed would be an understatement. Today's events had left her with emotional whiplash. Still, she couldn't say she was unhappy about what had transpired. She just needed time to wrap her brain around all of it.

She added parchment paper to the pans as the boys' laughter carried from the living room, making her smile. With Dad and Scott gone, the only man in the twins' lives had been her stepdad, Kevin. Now they had a dad and a grandpa to roughhouse with and teach them all those manly things she knew nothing about, and to be a guiding force in their lives.

Brady rounded the corner from the living room, then. "Anything I can help you with?" Pausing beside the counter, he eyed the rolls. "Oooh, my favorite."

She moved her neck from side to side, trying to work out the tension in her shoulders. "As well as your sons'."

"They obviously get their good taste from me." He moved beside her. "Your muscles knotted?"

"A little."

"As I recall, stress always hits you in your neck and shoulders." Behind her now, he settled a strong hand atop each shoulder and began to knead the taut tissue. "And I know you've had your fair share of stress today."

She rolled the triangular shaped dough, trying to remain calm. "How do you know that?"

"Because I remember everything about you." His warm breath on her ear caused her own to hitch.

Lowering his hands, he moved around her to lean against the counter, enveloping her in the scent of fresh air, hard work and something uniquely Brady.

She concentrated on the rolls, not trusting herself to look at him. Not now. Not today. She was too vulnerable.

"Thank you, Kirsten, for being a great mom to our sons."

Our sons. Hearing those words from Brady's lips made her pulse race. Something she quickly chastised herself for. She could not allow herself to fall for Jeremy and Trevor's father again. That would *not* be a good idea. She needed to stay strong. Because if Brady changed his mind, let his fears get the best of him once again, the boys would be devastated. And she'd be the one left to deal with the fallout.

"Mr. Brady?"

She turned at Jeremy's sweet voice, thankful for the distraction.

"Whatcha need, bud?" Brady knelt to Jeremy's level.

Finger pressed to his mouth, a sure sign he was feeling insecure, Jeremy said, "Can I call you Daddy?"

Holding her breath, she watched the two. Saw the way Brady's body relaxed, the sudden shimmer in his eyes.

He cleared his throat, nodding. "I'd like that a lot, Jeremy." Holding his arms wide, he added, "Come here."

Jeremy fell into his father's embrace, his smile somehow different. As if a part of him had been missing, and he'd finally been made whole.

The scene clawed at her heart. Brady had given Jeremy something she never could. Filling her with regret. Instead of entrusting her situation to God, she'd assumed control. And only now was she starting to see what that might have cost her.

Brady was doing this for his sons. But that didn't mean he liked it.

Sitting in a private office Wednesday afternoon, opposite a petite fifty-something woman sporting short brown hair with streaks of gray, he felt like a bug under a microscope. The unassuming, matter-of-fact woman had a way of coaxing things out of him he didn't care to talk about.

"I've never had a desire to know if I carry the Huntington's gene or not." Stuck in an uncomfortable armchair, he dragged his sweaty palms over his denim-covered thighs. "However, I recently learned I have two sons. Twins."

Behind a wooden L-shaped desk, Dinah—the woman who'd spent the last hour-plus going over insurance, his family history, his experience with his mother's Huntington's, as well as details about the gene and what he could expect moving forward—smiled. "Congratulations."

"Thank you." He stared at his boots that were usually reserved for church and other occasions where his worn dust-covered ropers weren't appropriate. "I feel I owe it to them to find out."

"Why?" Brow puckering, she cocked her head.

Because Kirsten all but demanded it.

Clasping his hands in his lap, he shook his head.

While she might have insisted, he'd come to the decision on his own. He hadn't been that much older than Jeremy and Trevor when his mother's symptoms started showing up. Both of his parents had been open with him about what was happening to her. Though, as a kid, it still hadn't prepared him for the reality. Yet somewhere in all the confusion and grief of watching his mother slowly slip away from them, he'd understood that it wasn't her fault. It was simply the disease.

Facing Dinah again, he said, "Because if I do have Huntington's, I'll be able to prepare my sons for what lies ahead. Both for me and for them."

The woman smiled. "I'm glad to hear you've put some thought into your decision. I'm sure it wasn't an easy one. Which is why many people prefer to simply let their lives play out without knowing. There's no right or wrong decision when it comes to presymptomatic testing, as long as you do what is right for you."

Once Dinah had informed him of what to expect going forward, he was given a folder with resources and information, and his next appointment was scheduled. Though the thought of meeting a genetic counselor, a social worker and a neurologist all on the same day had him feeling a little overwhelmed. But if things went according to plan, his blood would be drawn that same day, and he'd know for certain whether or not he had the Huntington's gene several weeks after that.

After locating his truck, he exited the parking garage and managed to find his way out of Houston's hospital district known as the Texas Medical Center, only to be met with bumper-to-bumper traffic. A powerful reminder of why he chose to live in the country.

Traffic moving at a crawl, he roughed a hand over his face, finding it hard to believe it had been just over two weeks since Kirsten showed up on his doorstep, telling him he was a father. And he felt as though he'd been on a roller-coaster ride ever since. Emotional highs and lows. Jolting twists and turns. Not to mention unexpected thrills.

That day he walked out of Kirsten's apartment, he'd built a wall around his heart. Fortified it, determined not to feel anything that could leave him vulnerable ever again. Yet with one simple question, a little boy—*his* little boy—had completely demolished that wall.

No doubt about it, Jeremy had something Brady didn't. Faith. Faith that a man he barely knew wouldn't reject him. Faith that he was worthy of being called son.

While Brady had that sort of confidence with his earthly father, he couldn't say the same about his Heavenly Father. The One who'd created him and knew him more intimately than anyone. Including Brady himself.

Except ye be converted, and become as little

children, ye shall not enter into the kingdom of heaven.

His grip tightened on the steering wheel. "God, forgive me. While I've never stopped believing in You, I haven't trusted You. Instead, I foolishly thought I could live in this bubble where *I* controlled everything. Yet You gifted me with not one, but two little boys. I know I don't deserve them, but I want to do right by them. Help me be the father You've called me to be for as long as You see fit. Help me to trust in You and not myself."

He sucked in a deep breath and exhaled it slowly as traffic picked up speed. "God, if I have Huntington's, I pray You will help me navigate the life You've given me as graciously as my mother did, and to start making memories—good memories—with my sons." A sob caught in his throat. "But if it's Your will, please, *please* spare Jeremy and Trevor from this awful disease."

Swiping the back of his hand over his eyes, he continued west on I-10, thankful to be moving at the posted speed limit. He took in the winter-weary countryside until he reached his exit, then continued onto the county road.

A short time later, his phone rang through his truck's Bluetooth. He'd been anticipating a call from his father wanting to know how the appointment went. Instead, Kirsten's name appeared on the dash, lifting his spirits.

Pressing the button on his steering wheel, he said, "Shouldn't you be seeing patients?"

"Well, hello to you, too." Just the sound of her voice made him smile. "And for your information, this is the first break I've had all day. We've had a steady stream of patients."

"That's great!" Each day seemed a little better than the one before. Monday they'd only had a handful of patients. Yesterday they'd almost doubled that.

"I know, right? It kept me from worrying about you." He knew he was reading too much into the statement, but the fact that she'd worry about him filled him with hope. "So how'd it go?"

"Overall, it was good. I think I have information overload, though."

Kirsten's giggle made him smile.

"My next visit should be loads of fun, too. All sorts of poking and prodding, both mentally and physically."

"You know why they have a process, right?"

"Yeah." The word came out on a sigh. "Though I don't understand why I have to know everything now. I mean, if I don't have the gene, they've wasted their time."

"But you're in a better position to understand things now than you would be if, or when, you learn you have the gene."

He chose to ignore the panic her statement

threatened to invoke. "I guess that makes sense. But I still don't like it."

"I know you don't. Real quick, are you going to want me to bring the boys over to help you with the horses, or do you want to come over after—hold on a second. I've got another call coming in."

"You got it." Tires humming over the asphalt, he eyed a modest subdivision that was under construction. Seemed the city kept getting closer and closer. He hoped those home builders kept their distance from Hope Crossing.

A couple of minutes later, he heard Kirsten's disconcerting sigh when she rejoined him.

"Everything all right?"

"That was the early learning center," she said. "Trevor is running a fever."

"And the urgent care center doesn't close for another hour. Do you need me to pick him and Jeremy up?"

"You won't be able to. My mom is the only person I've designated to do that."

"I would think they could make an exception in an emergency. You could call and let them know."

"No." She sighed. "I wonder if they'd allow Tori to retrieve them when she picks up Aiden. She could bring them here to me. Or maybe I can leave after I see this last patient."

She was willing to consider Tori, but not him?

"What if you have a walk-in? And what if

Trevor is still sick tomorrow? Who'll watch him then?"

Another sigh. One tinged with frustration. He'd asked too many questions. Still—"Kirsten, I *want* to help. Tell me what I can do."

"No, it's okay. Really. Don't worry. I'll handle it. I need to go, though. We'll talk later."

She hung up before he could say anything else.

He drew in a long breath. Kirsten hadn't even been willing to consider his suggestions. It wasn't like he didn't understand there were rules the childcare staff needed to abide by, but surely they could work with her. With them. Most, if not all, of the workers knew who he was.

Though they probably had no idea he was the twins' father.

He clenched his jaw, the thick layer of gray clouds suddenly mirroring his mood. Was that the crux of the problem? She didn't want people to know he was the twins' father?

But you're in a better position to understand things now than you would be if, or when, you learn you have the gene.

Or was she afraid to burden him because he might have Huntington's?

Rubbing a hand over his face, he shook his head. No, that wasn't it at all. Instead, it was her unwillingness to release control. And if she wasn't going to cooperate, then he'd have to force her hand.

Chapter Ten

Thanks to her appointment arriving on time, Kirsten pulled into the parking lot of the early learning center at 4:40 p.m. Small towns might not have the conveniences of larger cities, but at least you could get almost anywhere within a few minutes and traffic was never an issue. Which meant she could grab the boys and be back at the urgent care before closing time. Then, if she had any last-minute walk-ins, she could still see to them.

Easing her vehicle into a parking space, Kirsten recalled her and her mother going over every possible scenario that could prevent her from carrying out her duties at the urgent care *before* she accepted the position here in Hope Crossing. And while a sick child had been one of them, she'd foolishly assumed she'd have time to get to know people in the community and build a support system before the need arose.

How did the saying go? Hope for the best but expect the worst. If only she hadn't spent so much time worrying what to do about Brady.

"Brady." His name came out on a sigh as she turned off the engine. She'd been genuinely interested in his appointment and wanted to know how he was handling things emotionally. But that phone call from the early learning center left her reeling. Calling her mother was no longer an option. And Brady? Well, he had his own stuff to deal with. She hated to put any undue pressure on him when he was still processing the details of his appointment.

Besides, just because the truth was finally out didn't mean she expected him to drop everything and come running to help her, even if he had offered. She was used to dealing with the unexpected things that life with twins threw her way. He wasn't. Asking him to care for a sick child would've been like throwing somebody in the deep end when they barely knew how to tread water.

Wearing her white lab coat over teal scrubs, she hopped out of her SUV and hurried toward the early learning center entrance, wondering what she was going to do about work tomorrow. Even longer if Jeremy fell ill, too.

A groan escaped as she approached the door. Asking Mom to come down would be a huge imposition. But she might not have a choice.

She opened the door, her eyes widening when she spotted Brady talking with Alli near the front desk.

His gaze captured Kirsten's. "Here she is now." He smiled.

"Wh-what are you doing here?" She eased toward them. Had Brady told anyone he was the boys' father? Not that it mattered. Now that Jeremy and Trevor knew, it was only a matter of time before others did, too. "Is everything all right? How's Trevor?"

"He's resting in my office." Alli gave a reassuring smile. "But I think he'll be happy to see you. You know how kids can be when they're not feeling well."

"Alli was just telling me that you can designate anyone you want to pick up the twins." Brady's gaze was fixed on her. "It might be a good idea to think about that, so you'll have a backup."

Shaking off her insecurities, she said, "Yes. You're right. I need to do that." She brushed a loose strand of hair behind her ear and looked at Alli. "Can I see Trevor?"

"Of course." Alli motioned toward her office. "He's right in there. Would you like me to get Jeremy for you?"

"That would be wonderful. Thank you."

Kirsten continued into the small office lined with bookshelves, spotting Trevor on a small cot near the window. "Hey, Trevor."

Bottom lip pooched out, his cheeks flushed, he hugged his T-rex blanket tighter as she neared.

"I hear you're not feeling so good."

He shook his head, his gaze moving somewhere

behind her. "Daddy." The word came out as a pathetic moan.

While Jeremy had asked Brady if he could use the endearing term, Trevor had simply followed suit after hearing his brother use it.

"Hey, buddy." Brady squatted beside the cot. "I'm sorry you're sick."

Setting the back of her hand against Trevor's forehead, Kirsten knew some fever reducer was in order. "Can you tell me what hurts?"

"My froat."

She nodded, recalling the two cases of strep throat she'd treated this week. "We'll get you back to the clinic and I'll check you out, okay?"

Trevor nodded.

While Kirsten offered her hand as Trevor sat up, Brady held out his arms.

"Come here, buddy. I'll carry you."

When they returned to the reception area, Alli approached with Jeremy.

"Daddy!" If Brady hadn't been holding Trevor, Kirsten was pretty sure Jeremy would've launched himself into his father's arms. Instead, he rushed the man and hugged his thigh.

Though Alli remained professional, Kirsten noticed the slight widening of her blue eyes that now darted between the twins and Brady.

Turning so her back was to the boys, Alli cleared her throat as she moved beside Kirsten.

"Should I add Brady to the list of people approved to pick them up?" she whispered.

Kirsten darted a glance toward Brady. "Yes, please."

While he stayed behind long enough to give Alli his contact information, Kirsten took the boys back to the clinic where a luxury SUV waited alongside Dawn and Kara's vehicles. Must be another patient.

Kirsten unbuckled the boys, quickly formulating her plan of action. She'd settle the boys in the break room, then after she finished with the patient, she'd tend to Trevor.

Moments later, she opened the door to the reception area to find Dawn, Kara and a gentleman looking her way.

And as recognition dawned, Kirsten's heart dropped. "Dr. Olson? What are you doing here?" She cringed. Not the best choice of words when addressing one's mentor and boss.

The fifty-something gentleman turned her way. "You were informed we'd be making periodic visits. I was on my way back to College Station from Houston and decided to drop by." He looked from Trevor in her arms to Jeremy beside her. "I understand one of your boys isn't feeling well."

"Yes." She ignored the anxiety squeezing her chest. "I suspect Trevor has strep."

The door opened behind her, and she turned as Brady entered.

"Daddy." Jeremy cheered while his brother whimpered, burying his face against her neck.

Dr. Olson's narrowed gaze had her stomach churning. While he knew Kirsten was a single mother, she had yet to mention anything about the boys' father living in Hope Crossing.

"Hey, kiddo." Brady smoothed a hand over Jeremy's back and looked her way, concern lining his brow. "How's Trevor doing?"

"About the same." She cleared her throat. "Brady, this is Dr. Olson from our main office." She gestured and the two shook hands.

"Good to meet you," said Brady.

"Likewise."

"Brady is a deputy sheriff," she added as they parted. Since Brady wasn't in uniform, she didn't want her mentor thinking he was just any guy.

"He's also running for sheriff." Bless Dawn for adding that.

Dr. Olson looked her way. "As long as I'm here, why don't I take a look at Trevor?"

"I'll show you to an examination room." Her gaze inadvertently drifted to Brady.

"I've got Jeremy," he said.

Dr. Olson was all business as he assessed Trevor. And after administering a rapid strep test, he instructed Kirsten to give her son some fever reducer.

"Can I go see Daddy?" asked Trevor.

"Yes." She eased him from the exam table to the floor. "Do you want me to go with you?"

He shook his head and continued out the door.

Then, with a deep breath, she mentally prepared herself before joining Dr. Olson in the lab. In all the years she'd worked with the medical group, she'd never mentioned anything about the boys' father, other than that he wasn't involved in their lives. No doubt, Dr. Olson had lots of questions.

"Did you find everything okay?" She scanned the small space that also served as the pharmacy as she entered.

"Yes." The doctor faced her now. "Though that doesn't mean I don't have questions."

"I anticipated as much."

"We were under the impression the twins' father was not a part of their lives."

She explained the situation as briefly as possible, including the fact that she'd never told Brady she was pregnant.

"Kirsten." Her mentor gave her that fatherly look he had mastered.

"I didn't want him to feel trapped."

"Does he live here?"

"Yes."

"And you knew that prior to applying for the position?"

Her shoulders fell. "Yes, sir."

The man drew in a breath. "Based on what I

just witnessed, I'm guessing his reaction was not what you expected."

"No, not at all."

The timer sounded on the strep test.

"It's positive." The doctor looked from the test to her. "As we suspected. I'll call in a prescription. Just let me know where to send it."

Feeling somewhat relieved, she returned to the waiting room to find Brady holding Trevor in his lap while Jeremy demonstrated the train wall toy for his grandfather.

"Hank?" She joined them. "I didn't realize you were here."

"Someone told me our little buckaroo was feeling poorly, so I stopped by to see if you needed me to do anything."

Hands in the pockets of her lab coat, she said, "He has strep, so the doctor is calling in a prescription."

Brady tilted his head her way. "Do you need me to go pick it up?"

"That's not necessary. I can take care of it."

"Why don't you let me?" Brady insisted. "Either that or I'll keep the boys while you go."

"I have a better idea." Thumbs hooked in the pockets of his jeans, Hank looked her way. "Young lady, your plate is plenty full without adding to it. You go on home with the boys and let me pick up Trevor's medicine. I assume they'll allow that."

"Yes, but—"

Hank held up a hand. "No buts about it." The expression on his weathered face left no room for question. And she loved him for it.

"All right, but on one condition." She smiled as he arched one bushy brow. "You join us for dinner. I've got a big batch of white bean chicken chili in the slow cooker, so there's more than enough to go around."

His appreciative smile reminded her of the boys'.

Dr. Olson joined them, wearing a goofy smile. "Kirsten, I am so glad there's someone here who's not afraid to put you in your place." Moving beside her, he bumped her elbow with his own. "You do an excellent job of caring for others, young lady, but you can't be everything to everyone."

"That's what I've been trying to tell her." Brady shook his head.

"Accepting help is not a sign of weakness," the doctor continued. "And the sooner you embrace that truth, the easier your life will be."

"That reminds me." Hank's brow knitted. "Isn't there some rule about kiddos not being able to go back to school until they've been fever free for twenty-four hours?"

"Yes." And calling her mother was her only option. She'd have to pray Mom would be able to break away.

"Unless you've made other plans," said Hank, "I'd be happy to keep Trevor tomorrow."

"Oh, I couldn't—"

Hank's hand went up again. "Kirsten, like it or not, we're family now, and families help each other. I know how to take care of a sick child. And I'd be right honored for the opportunity to spend some time with my grandson."

Kirsten found herself blinking rapidly. Obviously, Brady wasn't the only one who wanted a relationship with the boys.

The thought had her cringing. How horrible a person was she that she'd denied these two wonderful men the opportunity to know their sons and grandsons? And more importantly, to have kept the boys from knowing *them.*

Her boys needed these men in their lives. And she was coming to realize, maybe she did, too.

By Saturday, life was returning to normal. Trevor was back to 100 percent, Jeremy had managed to avoid getting sick at all and Brady was looking forward to spending the entire weekend with them and their beautiful mother.

Now, as he sat across from Kirsten at her kitchen table just after nine on Saturday morning, still wearing his lined Carhartt coat, sipping a cup of coffee while his pajama-clad boys munched their cereal on either side of him, he found himself wishing every day could start this way. Strange how it felt so right.

Fingers wrapped around his mug, he leaned forward, resting his arms atop the table. "So, what would you boys like to do today?"

"Can we ride the horseys?" Jeremy grinned.

"Yeah!" Trevor's eyes widened.

Brady glanced out the sliding patio door and shivered. It had turned cold again, and temps were supposed to remain right around the freezing mark today. Thankfully, they weren't expecting any precipitation.

"It's kind of chilly for that."

"We can wear our coats," Trevor said around a mouthful of whatever sort of breakfast puffs he was enjoying.

"Not today, boys." Wearing jeans and a sweater, Kirsten stood, taking her empty oatmeal bowl and #1 Mom coffee mug with her as she scuffed toward the kitchen in her fuzzy slippers. "This is an indoor kind of day." She set the bowl in the sink and filled it with water before reaching for the coffeepot. "Now that I think about it, this would be a good time to do some prep for next week's bash." She refilled her cup. "After all, the clock is ticking." Gesturing with the carafe in her hand, she looked Brady's way. "Would you like some more?"

"Yes. And that's a good idea." He watched as she approached. "We need to get the horse heads cut out."

She topped off his cup. "I had a great idea to make them a little more horselike, but it'll take a little extra work."

Peering up at her, he felt his brow lift. "Such as?"

"If we punch holes along the head and neck, we can tie some yarn on them, and it'll look like a mane."

"I like that." Nodding, he glanced at the boys. "Though it's not exactly a kid-friendly project. Perhaps the boys and I should run over to Plowman's and pick up the yardsticks."

"That's wonderful they were willing to donate those." After returning the pot to the warmer, she rejoined them.

"They're good about stuff like that." His phone buzzed and he retrieved it from inside his coat. "Excuse me." He tapped the screen before placing the phone to his ear. "Hey, Dad. What's up?"

"Peggy Stallings called." The statement had Brady lifting a brow. This wasn't the first time he'd heard his father mention doing something with Peggy, a widow and Tori's mother-in-law. "She's taking her grandson, Aiden, to some new kids' movie in Brenham this afternoon and asked if I'd like to tag along. I thought, since the boys are friends with Aiden, they might like to come, too. Or, for that matter, the whole lot of you could come along. We'll be heading out around noon."

It would prevent the boys from being cooped up in the house. "Let me check and I'll get back to you in a few." He needed to check with Kirsten first, and she'd have his head if he tossed out the offer in front of the boys.

Kirsten watched him as he ended the call. "Everything all right?"

"Yeah." Twisting, he pushed out of his chair. "Hey, would you mind showing me that template for the horse heads?"

"Sure." She stood. "They're in the laundry room." When she started that way, he followed after her.

Once out the boys' line of sight, he touched her elbow. She turned, nearly colliding with him. Man, did she smell good.

Keeping his voice low, he said, "Sorry, that was just a ploy to get you away from the boys." He relayed the information his father had given him.

"That's a great idea." The way her eyes sparkled made it hard to look away. "What time?"

"He said they'd be leaving around noon."

"That should give you time to run to Plowman's while I work on the horse heads."

"You're really excited about these stick horses, aren't you?" He pointed to the stack on the dryer.

Squaring her shoulders, she sent him a saucy smile. "As a matter of fact, I am."

Aside from catching a glimpse of the old Kirsten, the fact that she liked his idea had him standing a little taller.

Naturally, the boys were thrilled to learn about the movie. So with the added impetus of a trip to Plowman's, they were dressed and ready to go in short order. And by the time they returned,

Kirsten had added brown yarn manes to the red, yellow, purple, blue and green silhouettes.

"Those look *way* better than the ones I showed you pictures of," he said.

She bit her bottom lip. "Do you think the kids will like them? I mean, they're not too cartoonish, are they?"

"Not at all." He inched closer. "Thank you for doing this. And for helping me. I really appreciate it."

"You're welcome. I like having a creative outlet." Her eyes went wide. "Oh, and wait until you see what I ordered. They're supposed to be here Monday." She peered around him, as if making sure no one else could hear. "I found some old-timey sheriff badge stickers I thought the kids might get a kick out of." Her grin wide, she playfully clapped her hands.

This was the Kirsten he remembered. The one who took joy in life's simple pleasures. The one he'd fallen in love with. And he was excited to spend the entire day with her.

"Get your coats, boys." Kirsten gathered up the horse heads just after eleven thirty. "It's almost time to go." She tucked them in the laundry room as Brady's phone rang.

One of his fellow deputies. "Hello."

"Brady. Glad I caught you." His friend sighed. "We have a situation."

"What sort of situation?"

"A neglected horse. It's in pretty bad shape."

Brady pinched the bridge of his nose. Not now. Not today. "How bad?"

"Emaciated."

That meant the animal had no insulation against this cold. And temps were expected to drop into the low twenties tonight.

"You interested in helping, Brady?"

"Always."

"You got the space?"

He heard the twins' excited voices coming from the living room. Along with other voices. Including his father.

"Yeah. Hey, let me call you right back." Ending the call, he moved into the living room where his dad, Peggy and an excited Aiden waited alongside Kirsten and the boys, their smiles eager. "Did I miss something? I just assumed we were meeting at the theater."

"We were," his father said. "But Aiden here got so excited when he found out Jeremy and Trevor were going to be there, he asked if they could ride together." The man's smile faltered then. "What's wrong, son?"

He gestured his phone. "They've got a starving horse they want me to come and get." Annoyance had him giving little thought to his choice of words.

"Starving?" Kirsten looked at him, her eyes wide. "How could someone do that to one of God's creatures?"

He shook his head, wondering the same thing.

"Brady, you have to go." Her hazel eyes bore into him, as though he were some sort of super-hero.

"I know." But he didn't want her to think he was ditching them. "I was really looking forward to spending the day with you and the boys, though."

She glanced at Jeremy and Trevor, playing with Aiden near the fireplace. "It's just a movie. Be-tween that and Aiden, they'll be so preoccupied, they won't even notice you're gone. And then they can tell you all about it later."

While her words eased his guilt, he was still disappointed. "Thanks for understanding." Join-ing the boys, he knelt to their level. "Hey, guys. There's a horse that needs my help, so I'm afraid I'm going to have to miss the movie."

"Is the horse sick like I was?" Trevor asked.

"Yes, but much worse."

"Then you have to help it get better," said Jeremy.

Brady couldn't help smiling. "You guys are the best, you know that?" He hugged them. "Have fun with Aiden, okay?"

"We will," they responded collectively.

As they left the house, disappointment settled in Brady's gut. Just a couple of hours ago he was thinking how they felt like a family. Now they were going their separate ways. Maybe this was God's way of telling him not to get too attached.

Chapter Eleven

The sound of three excited little boys echoed through the cab of Hank's pickup truck a few hours later. Since Brady wasn't joining them and the boys wanted to ride together, it hadn't made sense to take two vehicles. Though poor Peggy seemed to have gotten the short end of the deal, being stuck between Kirsten and Hank in the front seat.

Then again, after seeing them interact, Kirsten suspected the older woman might enjoy sitting shoulder to shoulder with Brady's father. The way Peggy's eyes sparkled when she looked at Hank seemed to hint they were more than just friends.

While the boys continued to jabber, Kirsten eyed the dreary countryside as Hank maneuvered the country roads on their way home, not recalling a whole lot about the movie. Instead, her thoughts had been with Brady, making it difficult to concentrate. She found herself wishing she were with him. Not that she could help all that much. Humans were her forte, not animals. Still, she wanted to support Brady. She knew how tough it was to care for someone who was in a bad way. How they might lash out or reject the help they so desperately needed.

Animals weren't so different. They, too, felt pain and rejection that sometimes left them unable to trust. But Brady was worthy of trust.

The thought had her heart beating staccato as they neared her driveway.

When had she begun to trust Brady again?

She mentally rifled through their interactions of late. Perhaps it was the humble look in his eyes when Jeremy had asked if he could call him daddy. Or the way he'd beat her to the early learning center when Trevor was sick. Maybe it was that day they were at the dance hall, when he said that kids may not have been a part of his plans, but they were a part of God's.

She shook her head as Hank brought the truck to a stop in her driveway and turned off the engine. Okay, so Brady had proven himself trustworthy with the boys. But her heart was another matter. She'd do well not to blur the lines.

Reaching for the door, she heard Hank call her name.

She turned. "Yes, sir?"

"You've been awfully quiet. Everything all right?" The knowing look in his eyes told her he had his suspicions.

"Of course. Just curious about that horse."

"Then why don't you run over to Brady's and find out?"

"Oh." She shook her head. "No. I wouldn't want the boys to witness something like that." She pushed the door open, then eased out of the vehicle and moved to the back door to free the boys. Before she could open it, though, Peggy took hold of her arm.

"Kirsten, Hank wasn't suggesting you take the boys with you." Her breath hung in the cold air.

She looked at the woman sporting a light gray pixie cut. "But—"

"We can stay with them while you go. They're already asking if they can play, anyway."

"I wouldn't want to impose on you."

Hank rounded the hood of the truck. "I would never think of my grandsons as an imposition."

Panic squeezed Kirsten's chest. "Oh, I wasn't— I mean—"

Brady's father chuckled. "I know what you meant, Kirsten. I was just teasin'. That said, why don't you get the boys unloaded and then you can run on over to check on Brady while we entertain the boys."

She smiled, thankful once again that he was a part of her life. "All right. But you'd better not let them eat a bunch of sweets." He'd brought them a month's supply of goodies earlier in the week.

"Oh?" Delight sparkled in his blue eyes. "Are there still some left?"

"Only because they're hidden. They've already had enough junk food at the theater. So when they claim they're starving, you can offer them string cheese, baby carrots or fruit, okay?"

"Bah. If you say so."

Peggy patted his arm. "He's such a softy. I'll make sure he follows through."

Once the boys and their booster seats were unloaded and inside, Kirsten changed into some clothes more suited to a cold barn. Then she told the boys she was leaving, but that Hank and Peggy would be there. Not that the kids really cared. They were more interested in playing with Aiden. Something that might have bothered her another time, but right now she was eager to know what was going on with that horse.

She texted Brady to let him know she was on her way, not knowing if he'd be too busy to see it or not. As she was pulling into his driveway, though, he responded, telling her to come to the barn, so she continued along the gravel drive, coming to a stop alongside his truck with the horse trailer still attached.

Moments later, she gripped the frigid metal handle on the barn door, her breath visible as she slid it open just far enough to slip inside before closing it again. The scents of horse and hay eased the tension she'd had all afternoon.

"Hey there."

She turned to find Daisy trotting her way while

Brady stood outside one of the stalls, a pitchfork in his hand indicating he'd been mucking the stalls. She rubbed the soft fur atop Daisy's head. "How's it going?"

He started her way, looking weary. "Slow. But then, situations like this usually are. How was the movie?"

"The boys enjoyed themselves. Giggled through most of it."

"And you?"

She scrunched her face. "Let's just say, my thoughts were elsewhere."

Nodding, he said, "I hate that I had to miss it."

She shrugged. "There'll be other times." Glancing about, she noticed all but one of the stalls were empty. The one that had always been empty until today. "May I see it?"

He leaned on the pitchfork. "It's not for the faint of heart."

"I'm sure. But I used to work in the ER. I've seen accident victims and I know how to deal with blood."

He glanced toward the first stall to her right. "No blood. Still hard to look at, though, knowing it could've been prevented." Leaning the tool against the wall, he motioned for her to join him.

Hands fisted in the pockets of her fleece jacket, she followed him into the stall. But one look at the animal had her pressing a hand to her mouth. Virtually every one of the animal's bones were visible, as though its scarred almost-black coat had been stretched over them, bringing the term "skin and bones" to mind. Never had it been truer.

The horse's unkempt mane was choppy, long in some places, short in others, and its black eyes were dull and vacant. It looked completely defeated, staring into the corner of the stall as though resigned to its pathetic lot.

She lowered her hand, her gaze continuing to move over the animal. "Male or female?"

"Male. A gelding."

"What can you do to help him?" She looked at Brady now.

"Coax him to eat small portions every few hours. Drink water. Gabriel—you met him at church—"

"He taught Sunday school."

"Yes. He's the town vet. He came out earlier and gave him a once-over." Brady stroked the animal's nose. "For the foreseeable future, the focus will be on getting him to gain some weight. Earning his trust." He lifted its chin. "Isn't that right, fella? We'll get you fixed up good as new. Just like the others."

"Others?" She looked at Brady. "I mean, I knew Butterscotch was a rescue."

He sent an easy smile her way. "Lucy and Digger are the only two that *weren't* rescues."

She found herself staring at him, stupefied.

"Brady, I had no idea. So, do you just keep them, or do people adopt them?"

"No adoptions yet. Though I should probably start thinking about that. Chief and Nutmeg are ready."

She continued to watch this man she once knew so well, realizing there was still a lot she had to learn about him. "I can't believe I never knew you were interested in doing something like this. I mean, I knew you enjoyed horses, but rehabbing them, that—" Showed a whole different level of compassion. One she'd convinced herself he didn't possess after he left her. "That's really amazing, Brady."

He shrugged. "Come here. I want you to show this fella some love." He took hold of her hand, guiding it toward the horse.

All Kirsten could think about, though, were the butterflies Brady's touch had ignited.

"Let him smell you for a moment." His voice was soft and low. "Now gently caress his muzzle."

When she did, Brady released her. And she wasn't sure how she felt about the wave of disappointment he'd left behind.

"That's how you start earning a horse's trust."

Trust. Funny how that word kept popping up in her thoughts today.

"Um, what time is it?" She stepped back as Brady glanced at his watch.

"Almost 4:30."

She felt her eyes widen. "Have you been out here the whole time?"

"Since bringing him back, yes."

"Please tell me you were able to grab some lunch. Or at least a snack."

He shook his head. "I couldn't bring myself to leave this guy just yet."

As a mom, she certainly understood that. Leaving a sick Trevor with Hank had been a challenge.

"What are you going to do tonight?"

"Probably stay out here. I've got a cot and sleeping bag just for this purpose."

How many times had he done this?

Perhaps for the first time since arriving in Hope Crossing, she was seeing Brady in a different light. He wasn't the cold, unfeeling man she'd made him out to be since he walked out on her. Instead, he was a compassionate, tenderhearted soul willing to sacrifice his own desires for the good of others. Including her. Something she hadn't recognized until just now.

Greater love hath no man than to lay down his life.

Yet she'd kept Jeremy and Trevor from knowing him, not to mention his wonderful father.

Shame descended on her as she shoved her hands back into her pockets. "I'm going to run to the house and fix you something to eat."

He placed a hand to his belly. "I guess I am getting kind of hungry."

"Kind of?"

"Okay, I passed famished a couple of hours ago."

Yet instead of leaving long enough to fix a sandwich, he'd chosen to stay with this creature who'd all but given up.

"In that case, I'll be back as quick as I can." Outside, the cold wrapped around her as she traversed the backyard toward Brady's house. But she didn't care. It was time she started showing Brady a little appreciation.

By Tuesday evening, suppers in the barn had become a regular occurrence. One Brady was fast becoming accustomed to. Not only for the food, but the company. Spending time with Kirsten and the boys had become as natural as breathing. If only there were more hours in the day.

Truth was there couldn't have been a worse time for him to take on a rescue horse. But thanks to the groundswell of support he'd received from his father, coworkers, friends and, of course, Kirsten, things had gone smoother than he'd expected.

After whipping up some soup and a grilled cheese sandwich for him Saturday, she'd picked up the boys and brought them over so they could continue their usual routine of feeding the other horses. While they did that, she tended the rescue he'd blanketed in her absence, not only because the underweight equine needed the extra insulation, but so they'd have time to prepare Jeremy and Trevor for the unnerving sight of a malnour-ished animal.

Later, his father relieved him and remained throughout the morning so Brady could attend church with Kirsten and the boys. Afterward, they'd spent the rest of the day at his place. The boys played and helped Kirsten tend the horse, while Brady made phone calls to line up help from friends and coworkers who'd aided him in the past. They'd come by to feed and evaluate the rescue when he was at work.

Yet while he was making things work, he still had the Boot Scoot'n Barbecue Bash to worry about, not to mention he'd all but abandoned his campaign efforts. Maybe next week he could find time to devote to that. Kind of had him wishing he'd gone ahead and hired a campaign manager. Until recently, though, he'd had an abundance of time. But that had changed the day he met the boys.

Not that he was complaining. How could he when he cherished every moment with them?

"How come this horsey doesn't have a name?" Jeremy asked as they sat on hay bales just inside the open barn door, enjoying the slow-cooker la-sagna Kirsten had brought. After a frigid week-end, temps had climbed into the seventies today. Yet while the air was still relatively pleasant, they were set to tumble toward freezing by morning.

Stabbing his plastic fork into the layers of pasta,

ground beef and cheese, Brady shrugged. "Good question." Probably because his main focus had been on keeping the animal alive. "Do you have any suggestions?"

The boys seemed to ponder his response.

"How about Rex?" Brady should've known Trevor would tie it to dinosaurs.

"No, Trevor. It needs a horsey name," Jeremy scolded.

Slipping Daisy a bit of meat, Kirsten caught Brady's eye. "How did you name your other horses?"

He lifted a shoulder. "They just kind of popped into my head."

"Well, given his dark coat, I think he looks like a Midnight," she added.

Brady and the boys cast her curious looks.

"Hello?" The female voice came from outside. "Anyone out here?"

Brady knew that voice. And it threatened to ruin his appetite.

Just then, Gloriana Broussard appeared in the doorway. Clad in jeans and a casual gray shirt, her smile faltered. "Sorry, I didn't mean to interrupt your supper."

Then perhaps she shouldn't have come by at suppertime. Or better yet, not at all.

"That's all right," said Kirsten. "There's plenty more lasagna, if you'd like to join us."

What was she doing?

"Thank you, but no. Supper's waiting at home. I just wanted to run over here real quick while Justin was available to watch Benjamin." She pointed. "These are your boys?"

"Yes." Kirsten sent him a wary gaze. "Jeremy—" she motioned to him "—and Trevor. This is Ms. Gloriana."

"Hi," said Jeremy, while his brother continued to eat.

"You've got your hands full, don't you," said Gloriana.

Stuffing his last bite into his mouth, Brady set his bowl aside and stood. "What can I do for you, Gloriana?"

"Oh, yes." Turning her attention to him, she lifted her chin. "I understand you recently acquired another rescue horse." She clasped her hands. "I'd like to help."

That wasn't what he'd been expecting. Another dictate about the big party at the dance hall perhaps. "Y-you would?"

She frowned, her brow puckering. "Why do you look so shocked? You know I love horses every bit as much as you do."

Yes, but the old Gloriana never would have made such an offer. That is, unless it benefited her in some way. "Don't you have to work?"

Nodding, she said, "I work from home and set my own hours."

"But you have a baby."

The eyebrow pucker was back. "Who's been around horses almost from the day he was born. I can always put him in his stroller."

"That's really sweet of you, Gloriana." Kirsten set her bowl aside and joined them. "This first week is going to be crucial, so Brady needs all the help he can get."

Arms crossed, Gloriana turned her gaze back to Brady. "Speaking of help. I haven't seen or heard one thing about your campaign. No signs, no emails, nothing on social media. You know, Brady, May will be here before we know it. Do you have any events planned? Because you need to be in front of the people."

As much as it irked him, she was right. "I spoke at a service organization meeting almost two weeks ago, and I'm speaking at a men's prayer breakfast next week." He wasn't sure why he sounded so defensive.

"That's a start, I suppose. But not nearly enough. Are you planning a fundraising event?"

He rubbed the back of his neck, keenly aware his campaign was floundering. "Honestly, I haven't had time to give that much thought since we last talked."

"Brady! You need a date and a location ASAP." She paused. "Wait! I have an idea. What if you had it at the dance hall? Let the citizens of the county see who you are, where you came from and still live. Show them that you're one of them, not some wealthy politician-type with lofty aspirations."

As if he had time to plan an event like that.

He rubbed the back of his neck. "That's not a bad idea." Oh, who was he kidding? It was a great idea. One he wished he'd come up with. "I just need to find the time to pull it together."

The corners of her mouth lifting into a smug grin, Gloriana crossed her arms. "Or I could help you."

His gaze narrowed on her. She could not be serious. Yes, she'd done a lot for the community, not only reviving the town's annual fair and rodeo, but taking it to new heights, enabling the board to make the improvements at the dance hall so they could have another stream of income. Not to mention how she helped save the youth group's Christmas Bazaar. Still...

"Look, I appreciate the offer, but I don't have a big campaign budget."

Shaking her head, she snorted. "Brady, you can be such a dork sometimes. I *offered* to help you. That means gratis. Free of charge."

His gaze narrowed once again. "You'd really do that?"

"Oh, good grief." She threw up her hands. "What is it going to take for you to believe once and for all that I have changed? Yes, I would really do that. By the way, I put a call in to the radio station. I'm just waiting to hear back."

"I'm finished, Mama." Jeremy showed Kirsten his empty bowl. "Can I have a cookie now?" She'd brought some of the goodies his father had bought.

"Me, too?" Trevor shoved the last of his lasagna into his mouth.

"Yes, you may. I'll get them in just a minute."

Trevor came alongside Brady then. "Daddy, can I check the horse?"

"Yes, but you're not allowed to go into the stall."

"I know."

"Can I go, too?" Jeremy looked so hopeful.

"Of course."

Kirsten gathered the now-empty bowls. "Excuse me while I clean up and get those cookies."

He watched her disappear into the tack room.

"Brady? Is there something you'd like to tell me?"

Facing Gloriana, he said, "Like what?"

She stepped outside and motioned for him to follow, continuing several feet from the barn before addressing him. "Did I hear correctly in there when one of the boys referred to you as *Daddy*?"

Lifting his chin, he glared down at her. "Yes. And not that it's any of your business, I had no knowledge of them until recently."

"How recently?"

"A few weeks ago." Not wanting to paint Kirsten in a bad light, he refrained from giving any further details.

"So *after* you decided to run for sheriff?"

"Yes."

"You don't owe me any explanations, Brady, but the voters will want one."

"I'm aware of that."

"Good. So." She crossed her arms. "Can I assist with the horse?"

"I guess I could use some more help. I'll have to bring you up to speed, though."

"I've got time." Her gaze narrowed. "And what about your campaign? You interested in some help there, too?"

He roughed a hand over his face, decades old hurt churning inside him. "The kid that still lives inside me *really* wants to say no." Under the barn light, he met her dark eyes. "But I've witnessed enough of your work to allow the adult in me to overrule him."

She smiled. "Good. Now why don't you show me that horse."

Without another word, he headed back toward the barn, praying he wouldn't regret what he'd just agreed to.

Chapter Twelve

Though the weather was cold and blustery the evening of the Boot Scoot'n Barbecue Bash, the Hope Crossing Dance Hall was warm and inviting as fair and rodeo board members like Brady scurried about, making sure everything was perfect as they awaited the onslaught of people that would soon be arriving.

The enticing aroma of smoked meat wafted through the large space, whetting Kirsten's appetite as she marveled at the hundreds, perhaps thousands, of tiny white lights that had been woven through the rafters enhancing the evening's festive ambiance. Long tables topped with black tablecloths and lined with chairs stretched to the left and right of the entrance, while the freshly refinished dance floor in front of the stage where the band was setting up glimmered beneath the overhead lights.

A dessert table boasting two large sheet cakes sat to the left of the stage, while the kids' zone had been positioned to the right, marked off with hay bales. Inside the space, two kid-sized picnic tables with benches had been covered with red-and-white-checked tablecloths and burlap runners. Small galvanized buckets held washable markers the kids would use to decorate their stick horse heads before they were attached to the yard sticks that were currently tucked inside an old milk can positioned next to a hay bale at the entrance to the kids' zone.

"This turned out so much better than I imagined." Brady stood behind her, the spicy fragrance of his all-too-appealing cologne wrapping around her. "And that's only because of you." He stepped in front of her, taking hold of her hands, looking breathtakingly handsome in a light blue button-down topped with a navy blazer that made those ocean eyes of his even more brilliant. "You took my simple idea and made it something extraordinary."

"We always did make a good team." The words spilled out of her mouth before she could think better of it. But then, Brady had always been able to distract her. Still, she wanted him to get all the credit. To endear him to the community and, in turn, boost his campaign.

"Yes, we did." Still holding her hands, he lifted them slightly. "I know I already said it, but you look absolutely stunning."

Her cheeks heated under his appreciative gaze. She'd worn her favorite party dress. A bright pink number with short sleeves, a fitted bodice and a flared skirt that was perfect for dancing. Not that she'd be doing any dancing. Unless it was with the twins.

Letting go of one hand, Brady gently twirled her with the other, making her skirt flare even more. And his smile had her tummy doing back-flips.

He's merely caught up in the festive atmosphere the same way you are.

Clearing her throat, she smoothed a hand over her skirt. "Thank you."

"*This* looks uh-mazing."

They turned at Gloriana's voice.

The woman wearing an adorable red peasant dress over a pair of white snip-toe boots was flanked by two teenage girls, one with dark hair, the other a blonde.

Stopping beside Brady, Gloriana scanned the kids' zone, her smile growing wider by the second. "How did you come up with this?" Her gaze shifted to Kirsten. "Or did someone else?"

"Oh, no." Kirsten held up her hands. "This was entirely his brainchild. I simply helped with the execution."

Brady eyed the girls. "I appreciate you ladies offering to help us tonight."

"Kirsten, this is my daughter, Kyleigh." Gloriana gestured to the dark-haired girl who bore a strong resemblance to her mother. "And her friend Callie."

Kirsten smiled. "Hello. And I echo Brady's appreciation."

"This is so cool." Callie wandered the kids' zone. "There's a little beanbag toss."

Kyleigh followed, pointing toward the corner. "And dart board." A sticky-ball one, anyway.

A beaming Brady joined them. "The idea is for the kids to have their own space, so they won't get bored hanging out with their parents." He picked up one of the horse heads stacked atop a hay bale. "In addition to the games, each child will color their own stick horse head with the markers on the tables." He eyed the girls. "Make sure their names are on them because they're going to be attached to these yardsticks." Pulling one from an old milk can, he demonstrated. "Then, before the dancing begins, we'll put those two barrels—" he pointed to the blue plastic ones sitting on the opposite side of the hay bales "—out on the floor so the kids can ride their horses in a good old-fashioned barrel race."

"Oh, I love that you tied in the rodeo theme," Gloriana lauded.

"That's such a great idea," said Kyleigh. "Can I make one, too?"

Brady's brow lifted. "Given that you're an actual barrel racer I'm afraid you're not allowed to compete, young lady."

"Does that mean I can?" Callie waggled her eyebrows.

Brady thought for a moment. "How 'bout you help any little ones who might struggle to do it themselves?"

The girl sent him a thumbs-up. "I can do that."

As the noise level began to increase, they glanced toward the doors to find them wide open and people streaming inside.

"Uh-oh." Brady checked his watch. "Looks like it's showtime, ladies."

"I will see you all later." Gloriana hurried toward the door.

Seeing the excitement in Brady's eyes, Kirsten couldn't help smiling. She nudged his elbow. "For a man who'd been uncertain about what to do for the kids, you managed to pull off something pretty incredible."

"I couldn't have done it without you and the boys. You inspired me."

"How so?"

"*They* motivated me to come up with something they would enjoy. And *you* gave me the confidence to bring it to life."

"I told you we'd find them."

They turned at Hank's voice to discover him and Peggy, along with the twins and Aiden, approaching. Since Brady and Kirsten had to be here early to make sure everything was ready for the kids, Hank had offered to bring Jeremy and Trevor.

"When do we get to color our horseys?" asked Jeremy.

"Whenever you like," said Kirsten. "Or you can play some games."

"Come on." Kyleigh held out a hand. "I'll show you."

The teenage girls were a great help with the kids, who seemed excited to have their own designated space. Some played games while others worked on their horses, all claiming theirs was going to win the barrel race.

Once everyone was inside the building, Gloriana and a pretty blonde Kirsten heard Brady refer to as Charlene took the stage to welcome everyone and bless the meal. And as some of the children rejoined their parents, Gloriana encouraged Brady and Kirsten to get some food and let the girls handle things for the time being.

They started toward the food line, stopping multiple times along the way. Brady seemed to know everyone, and everyone knew him. He introduced her to countless people, never failing to mention the urgent care center. So whenever the opportunity arose, she made sure to bring up the fact that he was running for sheriff. Something most everyone seemed enthusiastic about.

Brady remained at her side every step of the way, his hand resting against the small of her back. A move that was as unexpected as it was thrilling. And something she was determined not to overanalyze.

Once everyone had been served, Gloriana took to the mic again to let people know the cake had been cut and to encourage any little people who had yet to get their horse ready for the barrel race to do so now. That was Kirsten and Brady's cue to return to the kids' zone.

When it was finally time for the barrel race, twenty children ranging in age from three to eleven, armed with their stick horses, took to the floor. And while Kyleigh and Callie tried to urge them into a straight line, it was like herding cats.

Brady showed the kids how they'd ride their stick horse in a figure-eight fashion around the two barrels, amid chuckles from the crowd. Then he grabbed the microphone as Kirsten broke the kiddos into three age groups, the three-to five-year-olds going first, six to eight next, and, finally, the nine to eleven age group.

As soon as Brady hollered, "Go," rodeo music began spilling from the speakers. Callie and Kyleigh did their best to help guide the littlest ones through the maze, though their efforts were mostly for naught. Trevor's competitive spirit was on full display while Jeremy took care to do everything just right. But in the end, it was Jake and Alli Walker's little girl, Maddy, who crossed the finish line first.

The next age group took things a little more seriously, while the final group seemed to be playing for bragging rights. But it appeared participants and spectators alike enjoyed the festivities.

After a few more words from Gloriana, the band took the stage.

"Why don't I take the boys on home?" Hank hollered over the music a short time later. "Give you two time to unwind and have a little fun."

Kirsten handed him her key. "I won't be too far behind you."

Hank waved her off. "Take your time."

Kneeling to the boys' level so they could hear her, she said, "You listen to Grandpa Hank and do what he says." She hugged them before watching them disappear through the door.

"I think my dad might be onto something." Brady's breath tickled her ear and had goose bumps peppering her arms.

Daring a look into his ocean eyes, she said, "What's that?"

"About unwinding and having a little fun." He took off his jacket and draped it over the back of a chair before holding out his hand. "Care to join me?"

Her heart stammered. She'd always loved to dance but hadn't done so since they broke up. Being held in Brady's arms again could be a dangerous prospect. One too enticing to ignore.

She placed her hand in his and they quickly

made their way to the dance floor. Slipping into the crowd, they two-stepped around and around to several country favorites, Brady spinning her every so often. He'd always been a good dancer.

She'd begun working up a sweat when the melody finally shifted and slowed. Then the band began to play Kenny Chesney's "You Had Me from Hello."

Her heart pounded even harder. This was their song. Or had been.

Did Brady even remember?

Pulling her into his arms, he never said a word. Just held her close enough that she could feel his breath on her ear. How easy it would be to melt into him. It had been a long time since she'd been held in a man's strong arms. Even then, they had belonged to Brady.

He could still make her heart flutter. But that didn't mean they belonged together. Look what happened the last time.

No, they were only together now because of the boys. She was only here because she promised to help Brady. But, oh, how she wished this dance didn't have to end.

Ten days later, Brady sat at his kitchen table, still wearing his uniform, Daisy at his feet as he went over elements of his campaign with Gloriana. It wasn't the first time they'd met since the big party at the dance hall. The following Monday, she'd basically taken over the managerial duties of his campaign, freeing him up to focus on being the candidate.

"The fact that you'd done a lot of the preparation made my job easier. Now we need to work on the execution."

"Life kind of got upended when I learned about the boys."

She looked up from her tablet. "You really had no idea you were a father?"

Shaking his head, he said, "While I was upset initially, I understand now why Kirsten did what she did. We both made mistakes and have admitted as much."

"From what I've witnessed, you and Kirsten have a good relationship now." Gloriana grinned. "The two of you were awful cozy on the dance floor at the Boot Scoot'n Barbecue Bash."

The comment had his thoughts returning to that night. How holding Kirsten had felt so natural. Like she was made for him. And that song. It never failed to remind him of the first time he'd met her.

Scott had had to work, so Brady offered to pick her up at the airport in Honolulu. He was waiting in the baggage claim, and though they'd never met before, she walked right up to him, a big smile on her face, and said, "Hello, Brady." He was immediately smitten.

No other woman had affected him that way before or since.

"Kirsten has and will always hold a special place in my heart." Looking up, he saw Gloriana watching him.

"You love her."

"Aw, come on, Gloriana. No. Just because she's the mother of my children."

Arms crossed, she wore a cheeky grin. "You can deny it all you want, but you love her."

He cleared his throat. "Can we get back to my campaign?"

"Sure. If you can pull yourself back from wherever it was you went a few seconds ago." Again, she looked at her tablet, her finger moving over the screen. "All right. Fundraising event. I'll need to put together a press release for that." She looked at him. "I've reserved the dance hall for the last Saturday of March, but we need to discuss what time of day you want to have it so we can talk about the menu."

"I have no idea."

"Pancake breakfast or a dinner?"

"The pancake breakfast would probably be cheaper."

"Yes, but will it be as well-attended? Spring sports will be underway, so parents will have games to attend."

"Good point. Let me think on that."

"Also, don't forget the town hall at the Arbor-

ville High School the first Saturday in March.
That'll be a great opportunity for you to connect
with voters outside of Hope Crossing and give
them a chance to get to know you better."

"It's on my calendar."

She stared at her tablet. "Then I guess we're
done." Looking up at him, she said, "Back to the
radio interview." She'd spent the first half hour of
her visit prepping him for the event that was only
two days away. "Whatever happens, be thoughtful in your responses. Do not react, no matter
what they say. There are a lot of people out there
whose greatest joy in life is stirring the pot. Don't
let them get to you. That will only paint you in a
bad light."

He nodded. "Are we done, then? Kirsten is
holding supper for me."

Smiling, she pushed out her chair and stood.
"I guess it works out pretty nicely having them
live so close."

He stood, and Daisy did, too. "Oh, yeah. Seems
they're either here or I'm over there at some point
each day." Except for this past weekend when
Kirsten had taken the boys back to College Station
to visit her mother. Those two days had seemed
like an eternity. He'd missed the boys something
fierce. And thoughts of Kirsten seemed to play
across his mind every other second, reminding
him of how lonely his life had been without them.

"Hmm." Slipping her bag over her shoulder,

Gloriana eased toward the door. "All the more reason for you to pursue Kirsten. You obviously have feelings for her beyond being the mother of your sons." He started to object, but she cut him off. "I'm not blind, Brady. I've seen you two together."

He heaved a sigh. "It's complicated, all right."

"That's what people always say when they're afraid. Or the other person doesn't feel the same way. *Or* they've allowed some other ridiculous fear to skew their thinking." When he started to object, she cut him off. "I know this Brady, because I've been there. Justin and I had our own issues to overcome. But once we got over ourselves and admitted our feelings, we found it was easier to face our fears together than on our own. Kirsten has feelings for you. Feelings that go beyond sharing those two precious little boys."

"How do you know that?"

"Because there are some things you just can't hide." With that, she gave Daisy a pat and turned for the door.

Brady watched after her, wanting nothing more than to believe her. But she wasn't aware of the threat Huntington's might pose for him.

"Gloriana?"

She paused at the door. "Yes?"

"Thank you for helping me with my campaign. I appreciate everything you've done."

Her smile had the resentment he'd carried for far too many years fading away. "My pleasure."

After changing his clothes and feeding the horses, he said, "Come on, Daisy. Let's go see the boys."

The sun had already set by the time he piled into his truck. He sure was looking forward to some longer days. Temps had felt downright springlike lately. Even nearing eighty a couple of days. Which had been great for the rescue horse they'd finally named Midnight. Something that made Kirsten happy.

The horse was doing significantly better, eating as much alfalfa hay as it wanted both morning and evening. Though earning its trust would take a lot longer.

Pulling into Kirsten's drive, he couldn't help recalling what Gloriana had said. She seemed so certain that Kirsten felt something more than friendship toward him. After holding her in his arms while they'd danced, he knew he did.

Don't go there, James.

He stared at the painted brick house. The things he cared about most in this life resided in those four walls. This was where his heart was even when he wasn't. And that was a frightening thought. He loved Jeremy and Trevor with every fiber of his being. And Kirsten? Well, he supposed he'd never stopped loving her. But after the way he'd treated her, he'd be a fool to even think she'd return those feelings.

Daisy whined beside him.

"Sorry, girl. Let's go."

The boys had the door open as Daisy raced to greet them.

"What took you so long?" Trevor asked as Brady stepped inside.

"Sorry about that." Just inside the door, he scanned the living room, noting the dinosaurs littering the area in front of the hearth before realizing Kirsten was sitting in the chair near the door, her back to him. "Kirsten?" He moved around the wingback to stand in front of her. She looked exhausted. "You okay?"

A weary smile pulled at those pretty lips he'd thought about way too often lately. "Yeah." Standing, she stretched. "Just catching a little catnap while the boys played."

Daisy wagged her tail beside her, and seemed to smile when Kirsten petted her.

"Rough day?" he asked.

One shoulder lifted. "I didn't sleep well last night." She covered a yawn. "Dinner is ready, I just need to—"

"No, you don't."

Her brows arched.

"You don't need to do anything except sit back down. I can feed the boys. You're welcome to join us or I can bring you something and you can eat in here."

"We're not allowed to eat in the living room." Jeremy looked up from petting Daisy.

Brady smiled. "I know, but mamas get special privileges sometimes." He returned his attention to Kirsten. "You can even go to your room and take a nap, if you'd like. The boys and I will be fine."

She set a hand on his shoulder. "Thank you, but I'm fine. I think eating something will help reenergize me."

"In that case, you and the boys get washed up while I get supper on the table."

When she started to protest, he cut her off. "I know you're used to taking care of everyone else but let me take care of you for a change."

Her smile reached inside him and wrapped around his heart. "Thank you."

Soon, they were sitting at the table, enjoying the chicken enchilada casserole Kirsten had made in the slow cooker, along with a salad and tortilla chips. Then he helped her clean up the kitchen and played with the boys while she got their bath ready.

Once the boys were bathed and in their pajamas, they brushed their teeth before crawling under the covers for a story. Kirsten had a book of Bible bedtime stories she usually read from first before letting one of the twins choose a story. Tonight, they wanted Brady to read to them, something that always warmed his heart.

Finally, after multiple rounds of good-night

hugs that included Daisy and drinks of water, he followed a weary Kirsten into the living room.

"Now that they're settled, perhaps you should think about getting yourself to bed." Brady brushed the hair away from her face, foolishly allowing his hand to linger on her cheek. Her skin was so soft.

Leaning into his touch, she peered up at him with those captivating eyes. "Have I told you how much I appreciate you?"

He stared down at her, savoring her nearness. "No, but then, you didn't have to."

For long moments, neither of them made any effort to move. Until Kirsten pushed up on her toes and brushed her lips against his.

Instinctively, he dropped his hand, wrapping his arms around her and pulling her close. He kissed her back, fervently yet gently, breathing in the sweet fragrance of this woman he'd missed more than he'd allowed himself to believe. Her arms wound around his neck, her fingers soft against his skin.

When he finally pulled back, she rested her palms against his chest and smiled, her cheeks flushed.

He took a deep breath, leaning his forehead against hers. "And on that note, I think we should call it a night."

She nodded, her smile suddenly shy.

"I'll see you tomorrow." He kissed her again,

a quick peck this time despite the urge to linger. Taking a step back, he said, "Come on, Daisy."

Continuing into the night air, he couldn't help wondering if Gloriana might be on to something. That, perhaps, Kirsten did have feelings for him. And if they were entering a new chapter in their relationship.

Chapter Thirteen

Kirsten dropped the boys at the early learning center Thursday morning, then hurried back to her SUV, eager to hear more of Brady's radio interview. Jeremy and Trevor had been a couple of Chatty Cathys all the way into town, making it difficult for her to listen. They hadn't even realized it was their daddy on the radio until she'd pulled into the parking lot. Which, of course, made it more difficult to get them inside.

Now she started her vehicle just in time to hear the DJ say, "Welcome back, folks. I'm Tom Gentry here with Deputy Brady James, candidate for sheriff. Deputy James has been with the sheriff's department for five years, and I believe you went into law enforcement after serving in the United States Army, is that correct?"

"Yes, sir."

The sound of Brady's voice set her mind to wandering, as it had so many times since Tuesday night. Her cheeks heated every time she recalled kissing him. How pathetic was she that a simple caress had her throwing herself at him?

On the other hand, he had kissed her back. Doing a far more thorough job than she had. Still, it wasn't just his kiss that had her contemplating more what-ifs than a reasonable person should. Like the way he cared for the boys. His horses. Even her, taking control that night, giving her an opportunity to rest while he served dinner and then helped her with the boys.

No man had sought to meet her needs in a long time. Even then, Brady had been the one to do that. And he did it so well.

But did what happened the other night indicate he wanted something more than friendship from her? More than partnering to raise the boys? And if so, then what? Did she dare entertain the possibility?

Backing out of her parking space, she turned her attention back to the radio.

"It's also worth noting that his father, Hank James, was sheriff of this fine county for—" again the DJ seemed to defer to Brady "—what? About two decades?"

"Close to it, yes." Though most people wouldn't catch it, she noticed something in Brady's voice that hinted he was feeling a little uncomfortable. "He retired four years ago."

"We've got a few more calls here for you,

Brady," said Tom. "Ned, what would you like to ask Deputy James?"

She turned up the volume.

"We're having a problem out here off'a Shackelford Road with someone cuttin' our fences at night. Can y'all run some extra patrols out here so you can catch whoever's doin' it?"

Exiting the parking lot, she frowned. As if that had anything to do with Brady's campaign. The guy should be asking where Brady stood on the issues or about any changes he wanted to implement to improve their way of life.

"I will definitely bring that up to the current sheriff." Who, she'd learned, was also one of Brady's opponents. One more interested in his own political goals than the people of this county. "Livestock on the roads is never a good thing," he continued. "Especially at night, so I'll be sure to pass that along."

"Thank you, Ned," said Tom. "Now we move on to Bobby. What's your mind?"

"Your father was sheriff for a long time, and we loved him. But what do you bring to the table that would make you a good sheriff?"

"Excellent question, Bobby." She detected a smile in Brady's voice. "For starters, I've lived in Hope Crossing most of my life, with the exception of my time in the army where I served in the military police corp. I'm familiar with many of the people in the county and, like them, I appreciate our way of life. I also hold most, if not all, of the same values as my father. And I have no notion of furthering my political career beyond that of sheriff."

Oooh... Way to call out the current sheriff without mentioning his name. Good job, James.

"That's just what I was hoping to hear," said Bobby. "Thank you."

Kirsten made a left at the blinking light, followed by a quick right into the empty parking lot of the urgent care center.

"All right," said Tom. "Next up is Wilma. You're on with sheriff candidate Brady James."

Kirsten whipped into a spot, shifted into Park and listened.

"Good morning."

"Mornin', Wilma." Brady sounded as though he was finally relaxing.

"It has recently come out that you have two little boys. Twins, if I heard correctly."

Kirsten's smile flat-lined as the breakfast smoothie she'd enjoyed thirty minutes ago began plotting a revolt. This was precisely the sort of thing she'd feared from the moment she saw those signs on Brady's coffee table her first day in town.

"How come you didn't share this with the voters yourself? And if you weren't willing to care for your own children, how can the people of this county trust you to take care of them?"

Kirsten gasped, her heart pounding. She'd like to reach through that phone line.

Poor Brady. Having to deal with this woman. Kirsten's shoulders fell. Oh, how she wished she'd made better choices.

Without missing a beat, Brady said, "I'm not sure where you're getting your information, Wilma, but I'll be happy to set the record straight. It is true that, a little over a month ago, I learned I fathered twin boys and they have brought so much joy into my life. Being a father is something I don't take lightly. And while I haven't made any sort of formal statement, I haven't tried to hide this news, either. As you can imagine, I've been rather busy getting to know my sons and spending time with them. And from here on out, I plan to be fully invested in their lives."

Kirsten's heart melted. The same way it did every time she thought about that kiss.

"As for the people of this county," Brady continued, "they're going to believe whatever they choose to believe. But I pride myself on being a man of integrity, and that hasn't changed."

"Well, folks," said Tom, "we're out of time here at The Morning Roundup. I'd like to thank Deputy Brady James for joining us today. Up next, the farm report, followed by top of the hour news."

Kirsten sat there, gripping the steering wheel, her emotions all over the place. The smugness in that last caller's voice still had her hackles up. Yet,

Brady had come across as unflappable, handling the situation in a professional manner.

A knock on her window had Kirsten jumping.

Looking up, she spotted a seemingly vexed Dawn.

Kirsten killed the engine and opened the door.

"Were you listening to Brady?" The older woman's face was red.

"Yes, I was." Kirsten retrieved the backpack containing her laptop and lunch and slung it over her shoulder before stepping into the cool morning air. Thankfully, she'd told her staff about Brady being the boys' father not long after they'd disclosed it to the boys. Otherwise, she'd have found herself doing a whole lot of explaining today.

"People like that woman annoy the fire out of me." Dawn walked alongside Kirsten as they continued toward the building.

"You're not the only one." Kirsten unlocked the door and allowed Dawn to step inside first. "Would you mind getting things ready while I make a phone call?"

"To Brady?" Dawn's brows lifted as she peered over her shoulder.

The woman may be nosy, but she meant well. "Yes."

"Take as long as you need, then."

Inside her office, Kirsten closed the door and dropped her pack on a side chair before continuing behind the desk. Then she pulled her phone out of her pocket and dialed Brady's number, anger and regret volleying back and forth.

Two rings in—"Hello."

"I have *never* been so angry in my *life*."

"I'm sorry, Kirsten. I had no idea I'd get a call like that, but I tried to handle it as tactfully as I could."

"What are you apologizing for?" She paced the small swath of carpet alongside her desk. "*You* handled it just fine. But I'd like to wring that woman's neck. Trying to sound all holier than thou, all the while being a gossipmonger." Oh, yeah. Her ire was definitely getting the best of her.

And Brady's little chuckle wasn't helping any. "Take it easy. I've already talked to Gloriana. She suggested I make a video telling my side of the story so we can dispel any more rumors."

Dropping into the chair behind her desk, Kirsten sighed. "I've been worried about something like this ever since I learned you were running for sheriff. I feel like I'm the one who should make that statement, not you. After all, I was the one who chose not to tell you about the boys." Her shoulders slumped. "Now it might cost you the election."

"Kirsten, I appreciate that, but this is my battle to fight. You have the urgent care to think about. Besides, there's always going to be someone trying to cast doubt somewhere."

"Perhaps. But if I had told you about my pregnancy, you'd have one less battle now." Instead, she'd refused to give in to her mother's pleading and tell Brady. All in the name of protecting her heart.

In turn, she'd denied Brady the opportunity to know his sons, as well as Jeremy and Trevor knowing him. She'd trusted in herself instead of entrusting the entire situation—her heart, her life and the lives of her sons—to God. Now she was reaping what she'd sown.

No wonder Brady didn't want her help. After what she'd done, how could he ever trust her again? And the reality of that broke her heart far more than she'd ever anticipated.

The high school cafeteria in Arborville, the county seat, was standing-room only the first Saturday of March. Evidently, people wanted to hear what their local candidates had to say. Those vying for precinct commissioners and county clerk were all in attendance. Though of the three running for sheriff, only two candidates were in attendance—Brady and Garrett Butler, a forty-something state trooper who'd lived in the county less than five years. The current sheriff, however, was a no-show. That lack of respect for their constituents was only one of many reasons Brady hoped to defeat the man.

As a means to that end, Brady had been knocking on a lot of doors of late, introducing himself to residents. Between that, serving on the fair and rodeo board as they geared up for their annual event in June, not to mention work and the fundraising event, he'd had little time for the things he cared about the most—Kirsten, the boys and his horses.

What he wouldn't give for an entire day with them. Hard to believe it had been less than two months since Kirsten came to him with news that he was a father. How his life had changed since. Not in his wildest dreams would he have imagined his heart could be so full. God had truly blessed him. And Brady was doing his best to trust Him more each and every day. Even as he'd spent most of Wednesday in Houston, meeting with multiple professionals, including a neurologist, before having his blood drawn for the predictive testing. Now he waited. So it was just as well he had plenty to occupy his mind.

"Now we're going to turn our attention to our candidates for sheriff," said the president of the Christian women's organization. "Unfortunately, Sheriff Hulsted wasn't able to be with us today due to a previous commitment, but we are joined by Deputy Brady James and Sergeant Garrett Butler, so we're going to open the floor for questions."

Brady drew in a breath, his gaze searching the crowd for Kirsten. Fearful he might not be able to hold his tongue if things got heated, his father had offered to keep the twins, allowing Kirsten to attend in his stead. And just knowing she was there somewhere encouraged Brady.

Finally, he spotted her. And the way she smiled at him made him feel as though he could do anything.

Then he noticed the woman beside her, and his heart thudded against his rib cage. He'd once been close to her mother, Carol. Since Brady had been her last connection to her son, she would often call him when she was feeling down, and they'd share stories of Scott.

Then he walked out on Kirsten. And the phone calls stopped.

He could only imagine what Carol must think of him now.

Soon, hands were going up across the large space. One person was concerned about drugs coming into the county and wanted to know how he and his opponent planned to curb that. Another person was upset with the lack of investigation after a break-in at their home.

"This question is for Sergeant Butler. It has come out that Deputy James fathered two children out of wedlock and never acknowledged them until recently. What are your thoughts on that?"

Brady had to work overtime to remain unaffected by the half-truth. Yet, he managed to calmly turn his attention to his opponent.

The man shook his head, seemingly choosing

his words carefully. "From what I can tell, our opponent is the only one who is making this an issue. Deputy James has already addressed this, and I have no reason not to take him at his word. Like it says in the Bible, 'He that is without sin among you, let him first cast a stone.'"

The comment created a bit of a ruckus. Yet while Brady already thought the man a worthy opponent, his respect for Officer Butler had just grown exponentially.

"All right." The moderator raised her voice to be heard over the din. "We have another question."

As the voices hushed, he heard, "My name is Kirsten Reynolds. I am the mother of Deputy James's children and I'd like to set the record straight."

Murmurs started again as he jerked his head in her direction. What was she doing? Didn't she realize she was jeopardizing her position at the urgent care?

She went on to say it had been her decision not to tell him until earlier this year when she moved to Hope Crossing. As upset as he was that she would put herself at risk, it only amplified everything he already felt for her. Had always felt for her.

When the moderators finally wrapped things up, Brady could hardly wait to get to Kirsten. But there was one thing he needed to do first.

Standing from his chair on the stage, he turned

to his opponent. If today's event had revealed anything, it was how they almost mirrored each other on just about every issue.

"Good job, man." Brady held out his hand. "Sorry someone felt the need to bring you into my drama."

"Don't worry about it." The officer briefly shook his hand. "I meant everything I said. And if that's the only thing our illustrious sheriff can find to use against you, then he's grasping at straws. I think the residents of this county would be in better hands with either one of us."

"I couldn't agree more."

When he descended the platform, a handful of people stopped him with questions or comments. And by the time he finally made it to Kirsten, he'd forgotten her mother was with her. So when she moved past Kirsten and headed straight for him, his muscles tensed. After all, her daughter had just put her reputation on the line for him—the man who walked out on Kirsten.

Instead, Carol threw her arms around him. "It's so good to see you again, Brady." Holding him tight, she swayed back and forth. "How I've missed you."

Brady hugged her back. "I've missed you, too, Carol." From the day they'd met, she'd embraced him as her own.

Releasing her, he turned his attention to Kirsten

who waited beside them. "Though I have a bone to pick with your daughter."

"What?" She squared her shoulders. "I couldn't sit there and let them attack you when I was the one who'd put you in a difficult spot."

Setting a hand on each of their arms, Carol said, "Let's have this discussion back at the house. I'm eager to spend some time with my grandsons."

Brady was looking forward to seeing them, too.

"Why don't we pick up the boys and meet at your place?" Kirsten peered up at him. "I want to check on Midnight."

"Or I can call Dad and have them meet us there."

"Regardless, I need to change clothes."

While he liked the skinny jeans and flowing white blouse, they might not fare too well in the barn. "All right. I'll stop on the way back and pick up some pizzas for lunch. But we're still going to have that discussion."

The noon sun had warmed things considerably by the time they headed to the parking lot, making it a great day to be outside with the twins. Just as soon as he took some pain reliever for this headache. The tension of today must've caught up with him.

By the time he made it home, he barely had time to change clothes before Kirsten and the rest of them, including his dad, arrived. Good thing he'd gotten three large pizzas.

"Can we show Nana the horseys?" In the backyard, Jeremy petted Daisy, his blue eyes wide with expectation.

"I would love to see them." Sitting in a lawn chair, Carol straightened.

"We'll have to call them in from the pasture." Beside Kirsten, Brady polished off his third slice of pizza and was feeling much better.

"I'll do it." Kirsten set her paper plate aside and stood. "I want to check on Midnight, anyway."

Brady grabbed hold of her arm. "Not so fast." He glanced at his father. "Dad, would you mind going with Carol and the boys while I talk to Kirsten?"

"'Course not." He pushed to his feet. "Come on, gang."

While his father, Carol and the twins started across the lawn, Brady gathered up the spent plates and boxes, glancing Kirsten's way. "You, come with me, please."

Scowling, she followed him toward the house. "I never knew my mom used to call you."

He nodded. "When she was missing Scott."

"You were the last person to see him alive," she said. "I never realized how tightly Mom had clung to that. You were an important part of her support system. Until my decision not to tell you about my pregnancy stalled your relationship." Regret laced her tone. "No wonder Mom begged me to tell you." Kirsten shook her head and climbed the steps. "Here I thought I was *so* smart, never realizing how many people that one decision would impact."

He reached for the door. "Kirsten, that's all in the past. I want to talk about today."

With a huff, she followed him into the kitchen. "I don't know why you're making such a big deal about this. All I did was tell the truth."

"By throwing yourself under the bus." Setting the boxes on the counter, he tossed the plates into the trash before facing her. "You could've jeopardized your position at the urgent care."

She crossed her arms over her chest. "How?"

"You've seen firsthand how the rumor mill works in a small town. If someone decides to make a stink, you could lose your job and I don't want you to go."

Her wide eyes stared up at him for a moment, before darting away. "Don't worry. You'd still be able to maintain a relationship with the boys."

"It's not the boys I'm worried about." Grateful they were alone, he stepped closer, smoothing a hand over her silky hair. "I don't want you to go anywhere, either." Then, just to erase any doubts she might have, he kissed her. Not as thoroughly as he would've liked since someone could walk in at any moment, but enough to, hopefully, make his point.

He pulled away, smiling at her dazed expression. "Now you may go check on Midnight."

Chapter Fourteen

Kirsten waited for the boys to hop out of her SUV in Brady's drive on a Monday evening a little over two weeks later, noting that Brady's truck was absent. It was after six o'clock. She thought for sure he'd be home by now. Of course, he had promised to pick up pizza for dinner. Perhaps that was the hold up.

What if he's working late again?

He would've let her know. She pulled her phone from her back pocket. Nope, no messages.

Just as she was about to return the device to her pocket, it buzzed in her hand.

Got held over. On my way now.

She heaved a sigh of relief.

"Can we go to the barn?" While Jeremy had done the asking, both boys peered up at her.

"Not without me. Your dad's not here yet."

"Again?" Trevor kicked at a clod of dirt.

"It's not like he's doing it on purpose." Though

that didn't stop her from tossing the door closed with a little too much effort. Working late had become a regular occurrence for Brady since the town hall. And honestly, she was worried about him. The man had had too much on his plate for far too long. Now, in addition to work, his campaign, the horses and more, the sheriff had assigned him to investigate those break-ins someone had brought up at the town hall.

A move she suspected was politically motivated. As if the sheriff was trying to get back at Brady. For what, she wasn't sure. All she knew was that Brady was the one who'd responded to the person asking the question at the town hall, while the sheriff was nowhere to be found. Yet, Brady discounted her every time she mentioned it.

"Come on, boys. Let's go let Daisy out."

The Lab was more than happy to see them, nearly knocking Jeremy over when she bounded out the back door minutes later. The boys took it in stride, though, giggling as they chased after her.

Oh, to be that carefree. Instead, she was worried about Brady.

While he routinely claimed he was fine, the dark circles under his eyes and perpetually furrowed brow told a different story. And it was no wonder. He'd either worked late every night this past week or was tied up with some other commitment, leaving weekends to catch up on all the things he'd let go the rest of the week.

That only made her more determined to do whatever she could to alleviate even a morsel of his burden. Not only was it not good for him, the boys missed spending time with their daddy. She did, too.

Her mind drifted back to that second kiss and the words that had accompanied it. *I don't want you to go anywhere, either.*

She knew better than to read too much into it, but she couldn't help herself. Especially when her mother kept insisting Brady wasn't coming around just because of the boys. *I know that look*, she'd said. *It's the same one he wore five years ago.*

Kirsten snorted now. And look how that turned out.

If only those kisses weren't so few and far between, she might have a little more confidence.

She took in the pasture behind the house. The days were growing longer, and she couldn't help noticing the way the sun bathed everything in golden light. This was Brady's dream. Five years ago, it had become her dream, too. Until Brady crushed it.

Rubbing her arms, she looked to the sky. *God, I can't go through that again.*

She descended the steps and started across the yard toward the barn. "Come on, guys. Let's feed the horses."

Once inside the barn, she gave a healthy portion of alfalfa hay to Midnight before starting on the other horses' feed. What a difference six weeks under Brady's care had made in the animal. And though Midnight still had a long way to go, his eyes were brighter and there were hints that he might be starting to trust them.

Not so different from herself, she supposed. Not long ago, she wouldn't have trusted Brady with the boys, let alone her heart. Now?

Unwilling to answer her own question, she joined the boys in the feed room. "Oh, good. You've got their buckets ready to go. Well done, guys." Brady had written out what each horse was to receive on a whiteboard that hung on the wall in case she ever needed to feed them. Good thing, since this wasn't the first time in recent weeks she'd done so.

She wasn't complaining, though. Actually, spending time with the horses had become a high point of her days. They helped her relax. Most of the time, anyway. Tonight, she was worried about Brady and couldn't help wondering, if he were elected sheriff, how much busier would he be then?

Once she'd doled out the feed, she stacked the buckets and started up the aisle.

"What about our stool?" Jeremy watched her.

How could she have forgotten?

She set the buckets on the floor. "Standby, boys." Crossing the aisle, she took hold of the stepstool.

"Hey, guys. Sorry I'm late." Brady's voice startled her, making her lose her balance. "Whoa, there." In a single stride, he took hold of her arms and intercepted the stool. "You okay?" The warmth of his touch reached all the way to her heart.

"Yes." Regaining her wits, she joined him and the boys.

"Looks like you fellas have everything ready to go." He was still wearing his uniform. Something she found entirely too appealing.

"Mama did it," said Jeremy.

"But we helped." Trevor puffed his chest.

Moving beside her, Brady slipped an arm around her waist and captured her gaze. "Thank you for doing this." His bloodshot eyes suggested he hadn't been sleeping well. And it pained her to see him this way. She'd never seen him so overwhelmed. He was being pulled in so many directions. Trying to be everything to everyone. Never one to say no.

She found herself wishing she could make it all go away.

"Brady, why don't you let me and boys do the feeding while you go change clothes? Maybe grab a shower." *Give yourself a minute to breathe.*

"Ah, I'm fine." He waved her off. "Even better now that I'm with all of you."

She wondered if he was trying to convince her or himself.

"Did you bring the pizza?" While Trevor bounced with excitement, Brady's smile evaporated.

Sighing, Brady dragged a hand through his hair. "I'm sorry, guys. I was so eager to get home to you I forgot all about the pizza."

Why hadn't she reminded him when he'd texted her?

"Then what are we going to eat?" Jeremy shrugged.

Kirsten set a hand on Brady's shoulder, encouraging him to look at her. "Do you have any frozen pizzas?"

He shook his head. "A grocery run is on my to-do list."

A list, she imagined, that was getting longer all the time.

"How about this? You go change and freshen up while we tend the horses. Then we can go to our place where there are at least a half dozen pizzas in the freezer."

"Are you sure?" He frowned. "I mean, I can call in an or—"

"No. That'll take too long." Not to mention add to his stress.

Reaching for her hand, he entwined their fingers. "Thank you."

"You're welcome. Now go change."

Soon, they were caravanning back to her place. Yet while she'd hoped to alleviate some of Brady's stress, he seemed even more unsettled when he arrived at her house.

"What's wrong?"

"Nothing."

"Brady James, don't you *nothing* me."

He heaved a sigh. "Gloriana called on the way here. She needs some info from me for the fundraiser event this Saturday."

"Anything I can take care of for you? I'm happy to help you."

"Nah, that's all right. You've got your hands full, too."

"Brady—" she softened her voice "—you're pushing yourself too hard. You look like you haven't slept in a week, you're shaking." When he rubbed his forehead, she added, "And you've had a chronic headache for the last month. Your body is trying to tell you enough is enough."

Trevor peered around the corner from the living room. "C'mon, Daddy. Let's play dinosaurs."

Brady held up a hand. "I'll be there in a minute."

Trevor wasn't deterred, though. He continued toward them and grabbed hold of Brady's hand. "I want you to come *now.*"

"I said, no!" The vehemence in Brady's voice had Trevor taking a step back, his bottom lip trembling.

Kirsten glared at Brady as she reached for her son, pulling him against her. "I don't care how stressed you are, Brady. Don't you *dare* take it out on the boys."

"I'm sorry." His whole body trembled. "I—I can't do this." He turned then, his long strides eating up the distance to the front door in short order.

She heard the door slam before ever making it out of the kitchen.

Trevor began to sob. He wrapped his arms around her and buried his face against her hip as Jeremy rushed in from the other room, a stricken look on his face.

"Where's Daddy going?"

"I made him mad," Trevor sobbed.

Kirsten knelt then. "No, you didn't. Daddy isn't feeling well. I think he needs to be alone for a while." At least she hoped that was all he needed.

It was happening. The disease Brady feared lurked inside his body was finally making itself known. And he was helpless to stop it.

Even worse, he'd lashed out at Trevor. He'd made his own kid cry! Trevor had only wanted Brady to play with him. He hadn't done anything wrong. Yet, Brady spat the words out like venom. Who did that?

Now as he sat in his patrol vehicle the next morning, he felt as though both he and his life were falling apart. He'd hurt the people he cared about most. How would he ever make it up to them?

He snorted. Even if he had a clue, he'd have

to get past Kirsten first. He'd seen the fire in her eyes when she'd defended Trevor. She was a mama bear, all right. But then, a good father didn't speak to their children the way he had.

Parked near Hope Crossing High School, he took another swig of the lukewarm coffee in his travel mug and choked it down. Sure, it tasted nasty, but he needed the caffeine. Despite being wrung out, he'd barely slept last night. All he could think about was the look on Trevor's face when he'd yelled at him. Well, that and what his life was going to be like going forward. He may as well forget about being sheriff. Not when he might not be able to fulfill his commitment.

At this point, it didn't really matter. Without Kirsten and the boys, nothing else mattered. He loved them. Had actually begun to contemplate the possibility of a life with Kirsten. Then, in a split second, he'd blown it. Even if she were willing to forgive him, he couldn't reverse the Huntington's.

His radio went off. "Deputy James?"

"Go ahead."

"Possible hostage situation. Hope Crossing Urgent Care Center. Suspect is a white male. Mid-fifties. Brown hair wearing a ball cap, blue shirt and jeans. Suspect has a knife."

Four words jolted Brady from his sleep-deprived discourse. *Hostage. Urgent care*. And *knife*.

Kirsten.

"Copy that." He hit his lights. "ETA three minutes."

"Copy. Sending backup."

He stepped on the accelerator, his heart pounding. *God, please keep Kirsten safe. And help me. Strengthen me. Guide me.*

Though he raced into town, three minutes had never seemed so long.

Approaching the blinking red light, he tapped the brakes, checked for any oncoming vehicles, then made a sharp left followed by a right into the urgent care parking lot.

Dawn and Kara rushed toward his vehicle as he got out.

"Thank God you're here." Dawn heaved a sigh.

As eager as he was to get inside, to find Kirsten, he needed to know what he was up against. "What happened?"

"This guy came in wanting to see the doctor." Dawn sucked in a breath. "Kirsten, anyway."

"More like demanded," Kara added. "I should've known something wasn't right."

"What sort of treatment was he seeking?"

"He said he was in a lot of pain," said Kara.

"He waited for thirty to forty-five minutes, though, and seemed fine. A little fidgety, maybe, but that's normal when someone is in pain." Dawn waved a hand in front of her face. "After Kirsten joined him in the exam room, he started yelling."

Brady narrowed his gaze. "Did you hear what he was saying?"

"That he needed something now. That's when I opened the door to see what was going on." She huffed and puffed. "He yelled at me to get out. Kirsten told me to get everyone out of the building. He slammed the door then. That's when Kara called 9-1-1."

Brady ignored the panic burning his gut. Based on Dawn's account, he suspected the guy might be an addict. Painkillers, perhaps.

"Are there any opioids or other narcotics on the premises?"

"No."

While that was good, that could also infuriate the guy even more. Making him unpredictable. As if he wasn't already.

"I want you ladies to move a safe distance away from here." He radioed dispatch as backup arrived. Then he entered the urgent care while deputies surrounded the building.

"There's got to be *something*." A man's growl came from the direction of the exam rooms.

Brady eased into the hallway as silently as possible, listening for anything that might indicate where Kirsten was.

"We don't have any narcotics," he heard her say.

"Then write me a prescription," the male voice demanded.

Brady followed the voices. They were in the lab.

"I'm a nurse practitioner." Kirsten's voice quivered. "I cannot prescribe what you're looking for without consulting a doctor."

"So you're sayin' you're worthless?" The man's growl had Brady's back stiffening.

This was not good.

He inched toward the voices until he was able to glimpse Kirsten and the suspect, a man of medium build, approximately five-ten.

Retreating to one of the exam rooms, Brady spotted a metal tray. He grabbed it along with a chair and returned to the hallway.

"You can get help," he heard Kirsten say.

"I don't want help," the guy said. "I want relief."

With a deep breath, Brady tossed the tray. It landed with a loud clatter on the floor outside the lab. Then he picked up the chair. And when the suspect stepped into the hallway to see what had made the noise, Brady rushed him, knocking him over with the chair and sending the knife skittering across the floor.

Yanking the cuffs from his belt, Brady rolled the guy onto his belly before he even knew what had hit him and began reading him his rights.

"Brady?"

He glanced up at Kirsten. "Are you all right?" While she nodded, the way she rubbed her arms, all but hugging herself, suggested otherwise. It made him want to take her in his arms and assure her she was safe. But after last night, she'd probably push him away.

"We're going to need a statement from you." Eyeing the man on the floor, he added, "Why don't you join the others outside." He was surprised how calm he sounded when his insides were popping like firecrackers.

She looked from him to the suspect and back again, her brow puckering momentarily before she turned to leave.

Brady reached for his mic. "Suspect is in custody."

After hauling the guy to his feet, Brady escorted him outside, feeling as though his head were in a vise and someone was turning the screw.

Another deputy joined him, and they loaded the suspect into Brady's patrol vehicle.

Brady slipped into the driver's seat to start the engine, his heart hammering. Sweat trickled from his brow onto his cheek.

He stepped back outside. Temps were only in the fifties. He shouldn't be sweating. And why couldn't he stop shaking?

Things began to swim around him. He stumbled to the back of his vehicle, stooping as his stomach began to revolt. He couldn't catch his breath.

Something akin to a *Space Invaders* game darted through his vision.

He squatted, fearing he might pass out. A moment later, he did just that.

Chapter Fifteen

Brady hated hospitals. Even more so when he was the patient. Which he'd never been until now.

"You've been pushing yourself too hard, son." Late that afternoon, in an uncomfortable-looking chair to Brady's left, Dad leaned forward, hands clasped, elbows on his knees. "When you burn the candle at both ends, the candle burns out a lot quicker."

Brady rolled his eyes. He knew his father meant well, chalking what happened to Brady up to stress and lack of sleep, but Brady knew those things were just the tip of the iceberg. What they couldn't see, at least not until he received the results of his genetic testing, was the Huntington's that lurked beneath the surface, threatening to wreak even more havoc on his mind, his body, his life.

And just when he'd gotten a glimpse of the life he'd always wanted, yet never dared dream of.

Now his hopes had been dashed by the thing he'd feared most. And he had no idea where to go from here.

"Don't you see, Dad—"

A knock at the door had him turning that way.

Wearing the same deep purple scrubs she'd had on this morning, Kirsten poked her head into the room. "May I come in?"

Before he could say anything, Dad was on his feet. "'Course." He rounded the bed to hug her as she closed the door behind her. "How ya doin', kiddo?"

Glancing Brady's way, she drew in a shaky breath. "Better. Thanks to this guy." When Dad released her, she moved beside Brady's bed. "How are you?"

"I'd be better if I were in the barn instead of this bed, tethered to all these devices." He gestured to the blood pressure cuff around his bicep, as well as the IV pump and heart monitor beside the bed.

"I'm sure you would." The corners of her mouth lifted. "Speaking of the barn, the boys and I will tend the horses tonight." She glanced toward his father. "That way you won't have to hurry back, Hank." Looking between the two men, she said, "And what about Daisy?"

"She can stay with me," Dad said.

"Where are the boys?" Brady watched her cross and uncross her arms.

"Still at day care, so I can't stay long. I just wanted to see how you were doing and say thank you." She drew in a shaky breath. "I'm not sure what would've happened if you hadn't shown up today."

"Which begs the question, how are *you*?"

She gave a half-hearted smile. "I managed to push through. I think all of us were a little rattled."

"That's understandable."

Hands clasped tightly, she nodded.

Another knock sounded right before an aide breezed into the room carrying a food tray. "Suppertime." She deposited it on the bed-height table before making a rapid exit.

Hoping to lighten the mood, he glanced at Kirsten. "There's gonna be Jell-O on that tray, isn't there?"

She smiled. Nodded. "I'm ninety-nine-point-nine percent sure."

"And it'll probably be green or yellow," he added.

Puffing out a little chuckle, she said, "I wasn't aware you were so familiar with hospital food."

Whatever it took to see her smile. "I've heard stories." He needed to apologize for last night but wasn't sure where to start. "Kirsten. About last night. I'm—"

Another knock at the door.

They all turned as his doctor strolled into the room. "Looks like I'm just in time for the party."

"Sorry, I'm afraid I'm going to have to bow out." Kirsten backed up a couple of steps. "I don't want to be late to get the boys." The smile she sent

Brady was a sad one. Like a final goodbye. "You do whatever the doctor tells you, okay?"

Brady offered a small salute. "Will do."

With a wave, she disappeared out the door. And, probably, out of his life.

Meanwhile, the forty-something doctor with thinning hair stared at his tablet. "I have good news and bad news, Deputy."

Brady swallowed around the sudden boulder in his throat.

"The good news is your EKG was normal, and your bloodwork looks good." The doctor looked at him now. "The bad news is that you are stressed to the max."

Brady gave him a curious look.

"The headaches you said you've been having, the upset stomach, lack of sleep, irritability, they all point to stress and fatigue."

"What about the tremors?"

"I don't see anything that suggests Huntington's. How long ago did these symptoms start occurring?"

Brady shrugged. "A couple of weeks, I guess." Things had gotten worse since the sheriff assigned him to that investigation.

"I think the doctor's right, son." Dad inched closer. "Remember what I said about that candle? Your life today looks a lot different than it did a few months ago."

It sure did. Everything changed that day Kirsten told him about the twins.

"I'd like to keep you overnight," the doctor said. "Perhaps give you something to help you sleep. You look like you haven't done much of that lately."

Brady gave a resigned nod. He'd definitely need something if they expected him to sleep in this uncomfortable bed.

"All right, then." The doctor shook his hand. "I'll see you in the morning." He headed for the door. "Oh, excuse me." He sidestepped.

"Sorry, Doc." Brady's sergeant whisked past the man and into the room. Closing the door, he looked up. "Hey, there, Hank."

"Billy Rivers." Dad moved to shake his hand. "How you doin'?"

"Can't complain. Well, except for your boy over here." The man with a buzz cut and an average build poked a thumb over his shoulder. "Didn't you teach your boy that he can't take care of others if he doesn't take care of himself?"

Dad shook his head. "Deaf ears, Billy. Deaf ears."

"Okay, you two," Brady grumbled. "Stop talking about me like I'm not here."

"Did you hear somethin', Hank?" Sergeant Rivers grinned as he moved beside Brady. "How ya feelin'?"

"Like I want to go home." Back to Daisy and

his horses. Kirsten and the boys. He wanted to be with them most of all. But after what happened last night, he wasn't sure that would ever happen again.

"I hear ya. I just wanted to stop by and let you know I've taken you off the schedule for the rest of the week so you can have some time to recuperate. And if you need more, just let me know."

While Brady appreciated that, "What about that investigation?"

The sergeant shook his head. "I'm takin' it over."

"But—"

Sarge cut him off with a raised hand. "You're one of my best men, Brady. I need you a hundred percent."

Brady sighed. "Yes, sir."

"Now I need to get on home to supper." Sarge shook Dad's hand. "Always a pleasure, sir."

"You take care, Billy."

As the sergeant disappeared out the door, closing it behind him, Brady moved the table holding his food tray closer, suddenly curious. Not to mention starving.

When he lifted the lid, he couldn't help laughing. "Did I call it or what?" He pointed to the green Jell-O.

It didn't take him long to polish off every speck of food on the tray, including the Jell-O. While he felt guilty eating in front of Dad, the man assured him he'd be picking up a burger on his way home.

Watching Brady from his chair beside the bed, his father rubbed his chin. "I knew it wasn't the Huntington's."

"How?"

"Because I walked through it with your mother. From the first day to her last." He again leaned closer. "Brady, your life has undergone a lot of changes these past couple of months. You've embraced fatherhood and learned to balance it with work and other commitments. You did a bang-up job for the kids at the dance hall event, took on another rescue horse, had numerous campaign commitments, all while working to build a relationship with your sons." He lifted a shoulder. "Not to mention their mother."

Brady looked at his clasped hands situated atop the white thermal blanket covering his legs. "And I destroyed those relationships with one harsh comment."

Dad's brow furrowed. "What do you mean?"

As the blood pressure machine sprang to life, squeezing his arm, Brady told him what had happened last night. How he'd directed his frustration at Trevor.

"So you made a mistake. Parents aren't perfect. There were numerous times I yelled at you out of frustration."

"You did?"

"See, you don't even remember. But I sure spent a lot of time beating myself up for doing it. Parents aren't perfect, you know? I still regret sending you off to military school."

Brady shrugged. "I think it turned out pretty well."

Dad perched his elbows on his knees. "You know, Brady, when you decided to run for sheriff, you weren't aware of the boys. Perhaps you should rethink your candidacy."

"Folks will think it's because of a scandal."

"Who cares what other people think? The only opinions that matter are God's and the people you love. You love the twins. And you love Kirsten."

Brady wanted to deny it. But each time he was with Kirsten only confirmed what he'd been lying to himself about since the day she first told him he was a father.

"What if she doesn't feel the same way?"

His father shrugged. "Then you go on. I don't think that's the case, though. Even if she is mad at you, that doesn't mean she can't still love you." He looked Brady in the eye. "Son, what is it you want out of life? If you could arrange it any way you wanted, what would it look like?"

It didn't take Brady long to recall the moments he'd been the happiest in recent history. "Me, Kirsten and the boys would be a family. Doing life together, the mundane and the extraordinary."

His father smiled. "So what's stopping you from going after that?"

"You know the answer to that."

"You mean you'd rather let a what-if dictate your life instead of trusting the One who created you and living each and every day to its fullest? The Bible says that our lives are like a vapor. Appearing for a little while, then vanishing. Wouldn't you like that vapor to be filled with the people and things you care about most?"

Dad stood then. Stretched. "You're here for a reason, Brady. So are those boys of yours. It's no coincidence they and their mama ended up in Hope Crossing. They're here for a reason." He continued toward the door. With a wink, he added, "Think about it."

So Brady spent the rest of the evening doing just that, until his eyes began to grow heavy.

Lord, I gave You the reins on my life and then took them back. Now my failure to trust You might have cost me the thing I desire most. Kirsten. I love her. Show me what I need to do.

Kirsten stared at her reflection in the bathroom mirror the next morning, knowing there wasn't enough concealer in the world to tackle the dark circles under her eyes. She had barely gotten the boys to sleep last night. They missed Brady and wanted to see him. And the more tired they grew, the whines turned to tears and before she knew it, Trevor was having a full-blown meltdown, convinced that Brady was never coming back, and it was all his fault.

If Brady hadn't been in the hospital, she would've called or had a video chat with him. Not that it wouldn't have been awkward. Kind of like their visit at the hospital yesterday. Things couldn't have been any different if she'd been just a regular citizen thanking him for doing his job.

But there'd been so much more she wanted to say. Like she was sorry for yelling at him. And that she loved him.

Why hadn't she realized how frazzled he'd grown? She was a nurse practitioner. Instead, she sat back and watched—even complained—as one thing after another was piled onto his shoulders.

Yet, he very well may have saved her life. Seemed no matter what she'd said, that patient only grew increasingly angry, threatening her with that blade. Until Brady came to her rescue. At the risk of his own life.

Okay, so that was a part of his job. Still.

Her phone buzzed with a text.

Hank here. Didn't want to risk waking the boys by knocking. Mind if I come in?

Mind? He was exactly what she needed. Having him here would not only help the boys wake up but might help prevent another meltdown.

Wearing pajama bottoms and an oversized T-shirt, she hurried into the living room, unlocked the door, pulled it open and waved him inside.

"You have no idea how happy I am to see you."
She told him about last night.

"You shoulda called me. I'da been happy to
come over and help." After a moment's hesita-
tion, he said, "Brady loves those boys something
fierce. He's beating himself up pretty good over
yelling at Trevor."

"I didn't help things any when I got upset with
him." She studied her slippers for a moment. "Before he left, he said *I can't do this*." She made air
quotes with her fingers as she met Hank's gentle
gaze. "You don't think he was talking about fatherhood, do you?"

"No, I don't think that at all. He's just overwhelmed. Thankfully, his sergeant recognized
that, too, and insisted he take some time off."
He smiled down at her. "Don't give up on him,
Kirsten. Just give him time."

"Grandpa Hank?"

Kirsten looked toward the hallway to see Trevor
rubbing his eyes.

"Good morning, Trevor." Hank crossed to the
boy. "I came by to see if you'd let me have breakfast with you this morning."

Trevor's eyes brightened. "Really?"

"Yes, sir." He held out a hand. "Why don't we
see what our options are?"

Hank's kindness had her promising herself she
was going to do something special for him very
soon. Thanks to his help, the boys were in a good

mood and ready to head to the early learning center ahead of schedule.

After dropping them off without issue, she pulled out of the parking lot and was on her way to the urgent care when her phone rang. Anticipation rose inside her. Brady?

But her hopes were squashed when she saw *Mom* on the screen. "Hi, Mom."

"Just checking to see how things went this morning. Hopefully better than last night." She'd sent her mother a constant stream of frustrated texts last night.

"Much better." She turned on her blinker at the flashing light. "Hank came by to have breakfast with the boys, so they did great."

"What a relief. I was so worried they'd give you trouble."

As soon as she made the turn, she spotted a vehicle in the urgent care parking lot. One that didn't belong to Dawn or Kara. At least, not that she knew of.

"Have you talked to Brady?"

"No." She turned into the parking lot, her breath catching when she recognized the luxury SUV.

Dr. Olson was here.

"Mom, I need to go. I'll call you later." Ending the call, she eased into a parking space as an invisible weight settled atop her chest. She was about to lose her job. After hearing what happened yesterday, they'd decided to let her go. Why else would he be here?

With a deep breath, she gathered her things the same way she'd done every other day and exited her vehicle.

Dr. Olson stepped out of his SUV at the same time, along with another gentleman and a woman. They all wore grim expressions.

Swallowing the bile stinging her throat, she approached the doctor. "Dr. Olson. Good to see you again." She glanced at the other two people. "What can I do for you?"

"This is Dr. Cook, our clinical operations officer," he gestured to the other man, "and his assistant, Greta Ward."

Kirsten nodded to each of them.

"We heard what happened yesterday," Dr. Olson continued, "and wanted to talk with you before your day got started."

Tamping down her anxiety, she said, "All right. Let's go inside."

After depositing her belongings in her office, she joined the trio in the break room where one of them already had a pot of coffee brewing. The normally tantalizing aroma set her stomach to churning.

"Needless to say," Dr. Olson began, "we were quite worried when we heard what happened here. Thankfully, Kara kept us abreast of everything."

Still standing, he seemed to study her. "How are you doing?"

She took a deep breath. "I'm not going to lie. It was a little unnerving. But I'm doing okay. You know, that whole keep-calm-and-carry-on mindset." She cringed. Why had she said that?

"I can only imagine." Concern filled Greta's gaze.

"I'd like to commend you for instructing everyone to exit the building," said Dr. Cook.

Kirsten nodded, awaiting that big *but*.

While the other two continued to stare, Dr. Olson approached her as the coffee maker continued to gurgle. "Kirsten, are you going to be comfortable remaining at this location?"

Wait—What?

She lifted her eyes to his. "You mean you're not firing me?"

The older man looked confused. "Why would I do that?"

"Because of yesterday."

"You're not responsible for that man's actions. We're only here to make sure you and your staff feel safe going forward and to see what additional security measures we can take."

"I thought for sure—"

Dr. Olson held up a hand. "I'm sorry to have worried you. I should've explained myself up front." He smiled then. "But just so you'll know where I stand, Kirsten, the six months trial period is only a formality. As far as I'm concerned, this is where you belong."

Relief had her throwing her arms around her boss. "Thank you." Her cheeks suddenly warm, she stepped back. "Sorry. That won't happen again. I just couldn't help myself."

Dawn and Kara arrived while the coffee was being poured and after confirming they were also comfortable remaining on staff, Dr. Olson and his group set to work identifying areas of concern and how to address them.

To say Kirsten was relieved was an understatement. Now if she'd only hear from Brady. She missed him. But as hours morphed into days without a word, and the boys continued moping, she ignored Hank's comment about giving Brady time and decided to take matters into her own hands.

When lunchtime arrived on Friday, she drove to Brady's house. The man had been home from the hospital for two days and he had yet to contact the boys. Every time she looked at their pouty faces, her anger grew.

After barreling into his drive, she stormed up the front steps, yanked open the screen and pounded on the door.

When he opened it, she pushed her way inside. "You can walk away from me, Brady James, but don't you dare walk away from Jeremy and Trevor."

He backed up, appearing stunned. "Kirsten,

I'm not walking away from you or them. I've just had to take care of some things. To reprioritize."

Daisy whined beside him.

"Reprioritize? The boys haven't seen or talked to you in four days. That sounds more like a retreat."

He held up his hands as if warding her off. "Will you listen to me? Please? Then if you still want to purse-whomp me, you can be my guest."

She hauled in a deep breath and reached for her favorite tail-wagger. "I'm listening."

"After I was released early Wednesday afternoon, Dad took me to get my truck. When I got home, I tended the horses, made some phone calls, then crashed, and I didn't wake up until eight thirty the next morning. Then I met with Gloriana and Garrett to discuss withdrawing my candidacy and turning tomorrow's fundraising event into a rally for Garrett."

"Y-you withdrew your candidacy?"

"I was planning to come by to see you and the boys last night and tell you everything, but I fell asleep again, woke up at midnight, ate something, then went back to bed and didn't wake up until eight this morning."

No wonder he looked so well rested.

As her ire waned, she looked away, wanting to kick herself for not recognizing just how exhausted he'd been.

He touched her cheek, encouraging her to look at him.

"Kirsten, from the day I walked out of your apartment until you showed up on my doorstep, I've been going through the motions of life, ticking things off my list, as my dad is fond of saying, afraid it was just a matter of time before Huntington's caught up to me."

"I thought you liked being a deputy. And what about your horses?"

"Both of those things are important to me. But it was as though I were living in black and white. Unable to truly experience life the way it was meant to be. And then you exploded into my world again and brought more colors than I ever imagined. Everything—my job, the horses, life—took on a whole new look."

Lowering his hand to hold hers, he continued, "That day I was driving home from my first appointment in Houston, I recognized how far my faith had fallen. Yet God still saw fit to not only bring you back into my life but to give me two precious little boys. That day, I vowed to trust in God instead of myself. And to be the father He called me to be for as long as He sees fit." He paused then, his Adam's apple bobbing. "I stumbled a little Monday night, snapping at you and the boys. I thought the disease had finally caught up with me, but it turns out the shaking and headaches were stress-related."

She caressed his knuckles with her thumb. "You have had a lot on your plate lately."

"Which is why something had to give." He took a step closer. "You and the boys are what's most important to me. And I want to cherish every moment with all of you. So I withdrew my candidacy for sheriff and am going to encourage everyone to vote for Garrett Butler. I have every confidence he will make an excellent sheriff."

"I hate to see you give up your dream."

"I'm not giving up anything. At least, I don't think so. Instead, I hope I'm gaining more than I ever thought possible." Letting go of her hand, he said, "Don't go anywhere. I'll be right back."

She returned her attention to Daisy as he climbed the stairs, listened to the floorboards creak overhead, wondering what he was doing.

When he returned, he was holding what looked like a ring box.

Her heart rat-a-tat-tat-tatted.

"I know this is asking a lot, because we still don't know if I have the Huntington's gene or not, but I love you, Kirsten. Always have, always will. And whether I have five or seventy-five more years on this earth, I would love nothing more than to spend them with you. Will you marry me?" While her insides turned to Jell-O, he went on. "I'll understand if you say no or if you want to wait until we know for sure."

Peering into his ocean eyes, she smiled. "Brady, you're the only man I have ever loved. And I still love you. Period. End of story. I'm willing to trust

God to grant us however many days or years He sees fit. For better or for worse, in sickness and in health."

One dark brow arched. "Is that a yes?"

"Most definitely."

His kiss erased every heartache, every doubt she'd ever had. God had brought them back together in His timing, teaching them to cherish what was most important. Love.

When they parted, he held the velvet box between them and opened it to reveal a beautiful diamond solitaire in a yellow-gold setting. "This was my mother's ring." He reverently removed it. "You're the only woman I could ever imagine wearing it." With that, he reached for her left hand and slid it on her finger.

"Oh, my." She blinked. "It fits perfectly."

He lifted his eyes to hers, his thumb caressing her hand. "Kind of like us."

"I do have one request, though."

"Anything. Like I said, if you want to wait until after—"

She pressed a finger to his lips. "I want to get married *before* your appointment."

The lines between his eyebrows appeared. "But that's less than two weeks away."

She shrugged. "Take it or leave it."

His slow smile had her heart dancing. "In that case, whatever you want, my love."

Epilogue

Four months later

"Mama! Look!"

The excitement in Jeremy's voice had Kirsten looking up from her beach chair. The late morning breeze swept off the Gulf of Mexico, tossing her ponytail as seagulls screeched overhead, vying for the bread pieces Jeremy and Trevor were tossing into the air while Daisy bounced alongside them, barking at the birds.

Farther down the beach, Brady watched the scene, his heart full. This had turned out so much better than he'd imagined. While he'd been planning a daytrip to Matagorda in celebration of Kirsten's six-month anniversary at the urgent care, a random conversation with Garrett—who'd won their party's nomination in the primary election and, from the looks of things, was on track to win in November—led to an entire weekend at Garrett's parents' beach house. So, wanting to take full advantage of the weekend, Brady, Kirsten and the twins had driven down last night and awakened this morning to the sound of the surf.

He breathed in the salt air. God had blessed him beyond measure. Sometimes he still couldn't believe Kirsten was his wife.

They'd had a small wedding at the church the first day of April, then enjoyed a brief honeymoon at his farmhouse while her mother and Kevin took the boys back to College Station for a few days.

Since the only upstairs room he'd ever used for anything more than storage was the master bedroom, he and Kirsten had taken the time to assess the other two bedrooms, deciding the larger one would be good for the twins. Then they made plans to paint all the rooms, as well as update the bathrooms. Not to mention have all the original wood floors refinished. So rather than live amid the upheaval, they finished out the lease at Kirsten's until the renovations were complete.

As of two weeks ago, though, they were a hundred percent moved into the farmhouse. Though it may take them a month of Sundays to sort through their individual stuff and determine what should stay and what would go.

His toe nudged something in the sand. Kneeling, he picked it up, smiling. The boys were gonna love this.

"Hey, guys!" he hollered. "Come look at this."

Jeremy and Trevor abandoned the seagulls and hurried toward him with Daisy in the mix.

Kirsten pushed out of her chair, following them across the sand to where the waves met the shore.

"What is it?" Jeremy asked as Brady opened his hand.

"Whoa!" the boys said collectively.

"This is a sand dollar." He pointed out the petal markings on its flat roundish surface.

"Nice." Standing behind the boys, Kirsten smiled. "You don't find those too often."

"Can we keep it?" Trevor's eyes were wide.

"Sure," said Brady. "We'll add it to our other treasures." The boys had already collected numerous seashells.

Shielding her eyes from the sun, Kirsten gazed out over the water. "Uh-oh. Don't look now, boys, but here comes a big wave."

The twins squealed and rushed back to the beach while Brady hastily tucked the treasure into the pocket of his swim trunks before scooping his wife into his arms.

"Don't worry, Kirsten. I've got you." And he would never let go. Vowing to love her until death parted them wasn't something he'd taken lightly. Because while none of us knows how long we have on this earth, he'd known his time may be shortened.

Thankfully, only four days after they'd wed, the presymptomatic testing revealed he did not carry the gene that caused Huntington's. The disease he'd feared most of his life had ended with his mother.

Now he could only admire her valiant spirit, and live out each and every day to its fullest, just the way she had.

He set Kirsten's feet on the dry sand, his gaze drifting toward the dunes. "Dad and Peggy are here." The couple had driven down for the day.

"Yay, Grandpa Hank!" The boys cheered and hurried in his direction, Daisy between them.

After much prodding, his father had finally admitted he and Peggy were "an item." Brady was pleased. Dad deserved someone special to enjoy life with, and Peggy was a sweet woman.

"That was quite a welcome." Clad in a Hawaiian shirt and swim trunks, Dad carried two beach chairs, his smile wide as they caught up to Brady and Kirsten.

Wearing a big floppy hat, sunglasses and a sundress, Peggy peered out over the water. "I always forget how much I love the beach until I get here."

Beside her, Kirsten nodded. "I know what you mean. The sound of the waves is so relaxing."

"Looks a whole lot better 'round here than that parched land back home." Dad shook his head.

With temperatures hovering around the century mark for two months now, and little rain to speak of, things were looking rather grim around Hope Crossing. Sadly, the long-range forecast didn't appear to offer any relief.

"Y'all grab a spot and settle in," said Brady.

Kirsten touched his arm. "I need to run back to the house for a minute."

Something in her expression had him concerned. "Everything all right?"

"Yes." She nodded, her smile overly bright. "I just need to use the facilities."

"Ah. Okay. Bring some more waters when you come back."

She waved and started toward the dunes and the turquoise-painted home that sat just beyond them.

Brady joined his father in the surf to play with the boys while Peggy relaxed in her chair, her toes buried in the sand. But after a while, he began to wonder about Kirsten.

He glanced at his watch. She'd been gone twenty minutes. What was taking her so long?

Concern gnawed at him. "Dad, would you mind keeping an eye on the boys while I go check on Kirsten?"

"Sure thing, son."

"Thanks." Brady jogged across the warm sand and over the dunes, half expecting to cross paths with his wife. Instead, he approached the home that sat on stilts and took the steps two at a time. Yanking the door open, he hollered, "Kirsten?"

"In here."

He found her in the bedroom, sitting on the edge of the bed, staring at something in her hand. "Is everything okay? I didn't expect you to be gone so long."

"Sorry to worry you. I'm fine." She looked up at him, her smile wobbly. "Just a little taken aback, that's all."

"Why? What happened?"

"This." She handed him the blue-and-white stick she'd been staring at.

He glanced at it, uncertain what he was looking at. Then he saw the plus sign and his heart stopped. "I-is this what I think it is?"

"It's a pregnancy test. A positive one."

He felt the corners of his mouth slowly lifting. "You mean you're—"

"No." She stood. "*We're* going to have a baby."

Searching her hazel eyes, his heart filled with emotions he couldn't even begin to describe. "When?"

"That is yet to be determined, but I'm guessing early April."

"Next year?"

She laughed. "Of course, silly."

"I am silly." Tossing the test aside, he took her into his arms. "Silly in love with you." He lowered his head and kissed her, praising God for granting him a second chance. A do-over on the life he'd squandered out of fear. Now he could only praise his Creator, knowing he was fearfully and wonderfully made, just like Jeremy and Trevor. And this baby would be, too.

* * * * *

*If you enjoyed this book,
pick up these previous titles in
Mindy Obenhaus's Hope Crossing miniseries:*

**The Cowgirl's Redemption
A Christmas Bargain
Loving the Rancher's Children
Her Christmas Healing**

Available now from Love Inspired!

Dear Reader,

I hope you enjoyed another visit to Hope Crossing. From the moment I first met Brady in Gloriana's story, *The Cowgirl's Redemption*, I knew he was a wounded soul, though I wasn't sure why. And as God began to unfurl Brady's story, my heart broke for him.

Too often, when life gets tough, we fool ourselves into thinking we can do things better than God. But when it comes to diseases that threaten our bodies, only He is ultimately in control. The One who knit us together in our mother's womb and ordained all our days. The One who is worthy of our trust.

While Huntington's is a rare disease, if you've ever crossed paths with someone who's had it, you can't help but feel its impact. It's one of those things that leaves one asking why?

There's one more book to come in my Hope Crossing series and it's Tori's story. I know a lot of you have been asking about it, so I saved the best for last.

Until then, I would love to hear from you. You can contact me via my website, MindyObenhaus. com, or find me on Facebook—just search for *Mindy Obenhaus, author*. And don't forget to sign up for my newsletter so you'll be in the know about new releases and exclusive giveaways.

Until next time,
Mindy

HARLEQUIN
Reader Service

Enjoyed your book?

Try the perfect subscription for Romance readers and get more great books like this delivered right to your door.

See why over 10+ million readers have tried Harlequin Reader Service.

Start with a Free Welcome Collection with free books and a gift—valued over $20.

Choose any series in print or ebook. See website for details and order today:

TryReaderService.com/subscriptions